Advance Praise for

ALL THE NEWS I NEED

"This wholly original novel asks and answers the most urgent of all questions: how are we to live? In precise, pointillist prose, Joan Frank humbly delivers an unforgettable and unconventional love story with characters who both define and defy the rules of aging. Beneath the surface of these deceptively quiet pages lies a barely containable exuberance, a life-force I found moving and inspiring."

  —Christopher Castellani, author of *The Art of Perspective*

"Joan Frank is a human insight machine. In *All The News I Need*, two old friends, bound together by economy, loneliness and desire, travel through France. What ensues is life itself, rendered with subtle ferocity on every page. Joan Frank writes prose like no one else's—so psychically vivid it's like walking around wearing other people's minds."

  —Carolyn Cooke, author of *Amor and Psycho: Stories*

ALL THE NEWS I NEED

Also by Joan Frank

Because You Have To: A Writing Life
Make It Stay
In Envy Country
The Great Far Away
Miss Kansas City
Boys Keep Being Born

ALL THE NEWS I NEED

a novel

JOAN FRANK

UNIVERSITY OF MASSACHUSETTS PRESS
Amherst & Boston

ISBN 978-1-62534-262-1

Designed by Sally Nichols
Set in Alternate Gothic and Minion Pro
Printed and bound by Maple Press, Inc.

Cover design by Sally Nichols
Cover art: Cover photo: Two sitting at bench on a rainy day,
Image ID:75285766 © Masson / Shutterstock.

Library of Congress Cataloging-in-Publication Data

Names: Frank, Joan, author.
Title: All the news I need : a novel / Joan Frank.
Description: Amherst : University of Massachusetts Press, [2017]
Identifiers: LCCN 2016036159 | ISBN 9781625342621 (softcover : acid-free
paper)
Classification: LCC PS3606.R38 A79 2017 | DDC 813/.6—dc23
LC record available at https://lccn.loc.gov/2016036159

British Library Cataloguing-in-Publication Data
A catalog record for this book is available from the British Library.

ACKNOWLEDGMENTS

Full-hearted, full-throated thanks to first readers Ianthe Brautigan and Bob Duxbury; to the excellent Sam Michel, Carol Betsch, Karen Fisk, and everyone at the University of Massachusetts Press; to kind mentors, friends, and family who've never flagged, across the years, in their generous support, friendship, and faith.

For my cherished sister, Andrea Frank Carabetta:
held close for eternity.

Say you have seen something.
        —Annie Dillard, "This Is the Life"

Suppose you are like that famous wooden
music hall in Troy, New York,
waiting to be torn down
where the orchestras love to play?
        —Jane Cooper, "Waiting"

ALL THE NEWS I NEED

He thinks of chihuahuas when he sees a certain kind of man.

Then he always has to laugh. He laughs a little now, watching his boots move up the path. Breath comes harder uphill. Miniature cones, needles everywhere. Cypresses, redwoods. He slips through the flank of them, making for his bench.

It's Fran's fault, as usual. He heard her call them that once, and the image stuck. The bulging, leaky eyes; the slippery little bodies whining, shivering.

Oh, but *those* bodies—the ones Fran mocks?

Here we are. Unshat-upon, dry. Green paint not yet peeled off or carved into. He seats himself, tilts his head back, arms wide along the rim, closing his eyes.

European men on summer beaches. French, Spaniards, Italians.

Hairless, sexless. So Fran says. She'd seen them on the Italian coast.

Wearing those teeny bitty swimsuits that make their junk look like baby lightbulbs. I want to burst out laughing, she says.

She says *wanna*. He still envies the easy bravado in this: her slurry *r*'s.

Opens his eyes. Eucalyptus branches. Pearl mist evaporating as he watches, apertures of baby blue. Brine-breath from the beach. Medicine tang of leaves, acorns.

Rubs his cold hands. Should've used more lotion this morning.

Fran has pointed out that the beachboys appear not just oblivious of their effect: they are proud. Haughty as supermodels, turning their carefully browned bodies. This astounds her.

They don't realize they're hilarious, she says. What good is that?

Ollie sits up, yanks the windbreaker close. He'd never thought the men hilarious. He had envied and desired them all his days. Felt anemic by comparison. (Oh, he'd tried the protein supplements, chalky formula drinks, gym routines. Only in latter years had any flesh accrued, and then only in the little pouch above his groin: it made a lipless smile when he sat down.) But he came from such an ancient school of visual prompts. *Musclemen* had been the term, standing in for all the rest.

He shifts his ass on the bench. He has a bony ass, Fran once observed, after several glasses of wine. No buttocks at all, she said: his legs continue up to his waist, like a stork. She'd stated this calmly, with a scientist's interest.

A red-winged blackbird makes its elaborate call, a flutey bubbling, finishing just shy of a screech. Ollie's eyes race toward the sound and are rewarded: in the jade leaves a blood-red bolt, slash of molten lava against black velvet—then gone.

That red. Dear God. What could the species have had in mind?

He sighs. Of course: the female redwing.

When Fran mocked the beachboys Ollie had smiled in a puzzled way; it had taken time to grasp her joke. His old friend can say whatever she wants, because (she claims) she has moved well past *the time of caring.* When exactly is the time of caring? When we are younger, he assumes. But that's also supposed to be carefree. Sans souci. Except when had that ever actually been true of the young?

He strokes his chin. Remembers no time without cares. Worst in his twenties. If he concentrates he can still feel the waking moments, mornings in those years: spasms of hopefulness punching around in his stomach under a blanket of dread. He'd feared entering the world. He'd felt shamed, having no plan. Everyone else seemed busy at it—carrying out a plan. Important, urgent, outta my way. Everyone rushing around, rattling with purpose. No one spoke to him of doubt or difficulty. Many, surely, were pretending. He'd tried to pretend, but when he did he felt the falsity of it lump up inside him. Youth had shaped every care, for him, into an accusing portent. In college he could never escape the overpowering awareness he was a fraud, providing answers he'd been heavily tipped to provide, answers whose real significance in the living world remained withheld from him, answers he'd forget as soon as he'd uttered them. Nothing he studied sang to him. All of it seemed fossilized, distant; the languages of different disciplines alien and cold.

Loved French, though. Still does. Found it musical, wry. Still watches films to hear it, tries to follow it. Remembers clearly the day his freshman professor—an East Coast man (gliding along at the time, no doubt, on the academic conveyor belt to a cosseted niche in New England)—this man had noted, after Ollie offered some simple remark, *Vous parlez très bien aujourd-hui, Monsieur Gaffney.*

Some moments stay with you, pointing in a shivery way like a compass needle.

He'd stuck with the French. Even managed to slingshot himself to Paris the summer of his junior year, traveling standby—days of Pan Am and cheap deals—paying with saved slices of the living allowance his parents still gave him. Two stunned weeks sleeping in hostels, zigzagging around like a lost child, constipating himself eating bread and cheese. All he can recall of that time now is the damp smell of old stone, the bell-tower *bong* of train station announcements, the white-noise roar.

It hurts in his hip sockets, sitting in one position too long. Crosses legs. Recrosses.

●

He stands: dizzy a moment, pulsing roar of compensating blood in his ears. Presses his hands to his back, stretches his arms, pulling each at the wrist. He'll walk to the conservatory, get a coffee.

Air tastes sweeter with movement. Hup.

He'd liked some poetry in school. But it only seemed to make sense inside the cocoon of class. Once he stepped out into exhaust fumes and chrome it dissolved, and all the books he brought home resisted his wits: obdurate, seamless, like those smooth boxes that defied you to locate a sliding panel. He couldn't retain anything, but much worse, couldn't believe anything. What sank his belly again and again were the faces of his fellow students— tensed and twitching as if about to race, waiting for the boom of the starting gun. He'd barely crawled through and been graduated, essentially, as a courtesy. Though they'd never discussed it, he felt pretty sure his father had made a few phone calls, facilitating that. It was the same university where both his parents worked; tuition low then; he could still live at home.

Afterward he'd worked grunge jobs. Janitor, fruit-picking, gas stations, ticket-taking, refiling library books. Whatever job he chose, he'd always sensed, was an error, a meaningless postponement at best, though no one said this aloud. His parents' silence was hardest to bear. They kept quiet as they moved through routines, but the air around them clotted and cooled: no pounded gavel could have delivered the verdict better. They'd wanted him, he knew, to do what they'd done, take shelter inside the academy. Anxiety cooked in his stomach. He'd moved out, rented a room down the highway. An old fifties house, sharecropperish with small, square rooms, in the orchard town of Dixon, with a handful of other misfits. They were friendly but distracted; dragged themselves to strange jobs at all hours and smoked dope the rest of the time. Ollie found he didn't like the weed—it burned his throat and made him drool and cough, after which his thoughts grew more paranoid. He never confessed that. A tall, skinny kid with long feet, he'd had real hair back then. Shiny and straight, light brown, parted on the side. *Thomas Edison hair,* Fran called it, examining his old snapshots. Sometimes he would slip from the house into the hot, clear morning in just his shorts and stand barefoot on the front walkway staring at the foothills, pavement already warm under his soles. And though the setting was peaceful and by any standards beautiful, the only clear thought he could identify was a longing to disappear.

Days peeled off. The white noise of the wind, of cars roaring heartlessly back and forth on the freeway—these gave no instruction, made no comment.

He stamps along, listening to his breath. Light behind leaves, trees: green stained glass.

•

He'd sensed he was being watched back then, those painful years. Nothing you could prove—a kind of quickened vibration at his temples. Much later he decided it was a delusion common to people his age—the unspoken belief they'd been starring in an ongoing film of their own lives, playing round-the-clock to some mesmerized audience in a parallel universe. Later still, he recognized the same delusion in most of the young people he met: an opaque light in the eyes, as if hearing a set of secret instructions inaudible to all others.

Whatever he tried in those days, the more foolish he felt. As if at any moment the gods would sigh like a bunch of exhausted talent scouts, look at their watches, and yank him off the earthly stage with a big god-hook. No one admitted such fears back then. But he remembers waking in the morning, thousands of mornings, jaws sore from grinding teeth.

He ducks up the path along the ridge, behind the soccer field.

•

Touches the silver stubble along his jaw. Rough as wire, wiretips scritching the sworls of his fingerpads. Pushes his hands into his jacket pockets. How sturdy those wiry hairs. Tough genetic stuff. Leftovers from a hairy evolution, millennia of adrenalin-flooded scrambling up iced mountainsides with no more protection than a flap of animal skin and handful of homemade arrows. How briefly he'd have lasted! The hardiest man rarely made it to twenty-five. He'd have become someone's dinner in moments. Sheerest luck, born into a century of vaccines and vitamins, a warm, western city, some modicum of civil law. Now, anti-HIV cocktails. With a bit more luck, even marriage if you wished it.

He sighs. Late for that.

His pubic area is going gray. Silver, more like.

One hand floats up toward his chin. He shoves it back into his pocket. He needs to buy a magnifying mirror; shave closer. But then he'll need to install the thing. Probably take half the bathroom wall down. And who's he trying to impress?

Dating's over. Partners over.

Dry blond grass alongside, bowing like wheat.

Fran says the essential trick is that of impressing yourself. Staying upright, she calls it.

Fran's an amusing artifact. An *éspèce*. He is certain she classifies him the same way. Ollie the old queen, he figures she's dubbed him. Doubtless she said it to Kirk, at least at the beginning. The term a laundry chute, a little trapdoor where she tossed stray thoughts about him like unmatched socks. Fran practices survivor manners, which is to say, none. She plunks her shod feet on the dining table, laughs with a honk, swears graphically, drinks wine chased by beer from the bottle— lifted high with each swig, as if she were taking aim with a spyglass.

He now understands that much of her swagger functions as bravado, a kind of compensatory noise. She still carries spiders and ants—ants!—out of the house on a piece of tissue, apologizing to them while she moves them outside. (Why should they die? she demands. What did they do?) Gets weepy at the Budweiser ads with the Clydesdales, the commercials for diamonds. Still wears the modest ring Kirk gave her, ten microscopic stones in a gold band. From Macy's on sale, she'd told Ollie proudly. She'd simply pulled Kirk over to the store one day after she'd seen it and said, that one. The ring made both of them happy because it was, in her words, way cheap. Neither believed, she said, in that kind of spending.

Except for travel.

Passing eyes greet him pleasantly. He's among confederates

now on the wide Kennedy Drive, bicyclists, runners, baby-pram pushers. Above him, the blue hole in the mist opens wider.

Fran had been married many years to his old friend Kirkland, a genial history teacher Ollie first met—so long ago now—on one of those fly-to-Mexico-to-learn-Spanish semesters. Kirk had wanted simply to get out of town. Those were the years before Frannie, when he'd run through a series of horrific girlfriends—like being smacked over and over by a revolving door, Kirk said. He loved nothing better than clearing off, as he called it. Ollie had persuaded his bosses he'd do better with his Spanish-speaking kids if he got more practice at it—he taught preschool for a private school in Cole Valley. Deciding they could cite it at board meetings as evidence of the school's progressive mission, the directors let him take an unpaid leave.

Kirk, a jovial Fulbright transplant from Edinburgh, had a squinty grin, horn-rim glasses, a head of brass-colored hair rippling back from his brow in kinked waves like photos of physicists in the 1940s—and an appetite for alcohol and distraction that had elbowed Ollie out of his gloom caul (Kirk's term for it). Kirk had immediately established, when they met, that he was straight—but cheerfully, kindly. They were the same age, it pleased them to learn. And how relieved they'd been, the both of them, to make an English-speaking friend in that deadened outback!

Ollie folds his arms, leaning forward as he strode, smiling a little.

They'd rented rooms in splintery boarding houses, lurched around the desert on buses that never failed to break down—at which point a herd of weathered old women emerged from nowhere and began trudging toward them in the dust like B-movie zombies, holding out grimy religious trinkets to sell. The heat pasted his skin, Ollie remembers, stinging till you stepped into shade. He and Kirk learned to eat thin soup (bouillon really, with floating bits he didn't dare ask about). They walked around the tumbledown *zocalos*—more like ruins *manqué*. Poor Kirk kept inventing day-trips, pushing Ollie out the door on these fruitless expeditions—he'd longed to find, somewhere in Mexico, a cheap, warm, European *centre-ville*. Learned his error soon enough. After a period of hunting they'd give up and return to their rooms every night guarding only one hope: that someone would of a sudden, in the middle of dry deadness, yell *Fiesta!*— and then the whole household, no matter how dazed and dreary, would move fast. Floors would clear; cerveza or tequila (like turpentine) appeared, along with boombox music, pork rinds, peanuts (rancid, but they canceled the awful taste of the drink). The dancing and whooping (*Vaya, vaya!*) carried on all night, after which they'd step over passed-out bodies to crawl into their not-clean beds, sweating and stinking.

Many years ago.

•

(Skip the de Young and the Science Academy today. It's too lovely out.)

Kirk had met Fran in City Lights bookstore. They'd stood together in the *B*'s, Brautigan, Bukowski, chatting about their tastes, which *sort of coincided but mostly didn't,* according to Fran. (She claimed Kirk had mocked the writer Peter Taylor. Fran admired Taylor, but she also recognized a crude accuracy in Kirk's chiding—it made her laugh.) Then they sauntered down the block for a drink at Vesuvio's. Then up the block, for dinner at Calzone. After a couple of years she left the city to move in with him, an hour north. Ollie used to visit a lot right after Kirk died, but less over time. He sees Fran rarely now. She still lives in the little gray house on Dryden, the pleasant suburb.

Pleasant—a word that calls to mind precisely the wide streets, canopies of trees, long grass, poppies and roses and shade-protected ferns that surround the Ferguson place. The turned beds in the backyard where Kirk raised tomatoes have gone to wild mustard and herbs; a massive Japanese maple umbrellas almost the whole of it. Fran loves the tree so much she swears she wants to be buried under it. Ollie used to sit out there drinking wine with both of them in summer—day's end, when the heat inside the house was still intolerable. They would stay up late, citronella candle flames wobbling in the dark, waiting for the evening air to come close to bearable. Fran would excuse herself every twenty minutes to take cold showers. After each shower, she told them, the air felt dreamy for two minutes—all the towels pre-warmed, she said—then the heat closed back over. Kirk was still smoking cigars then. Fran finally forbade this, locking eyes with her husband if she suspected him of even thinking about it.

All bets are off at their ages, she'd remind him.

Yes—dear, Kirk would answer in robot monotones, rolling his eyes at Ollie.

Fran did, of course, have a point. All of them were losing people by then—many more since. Starting with Kirk himself, eight years ago, to an utterly mundane and yet too-predictable stroke. (Ollie gave secret, silent thanks it had been swift—everyone by then knowing horrible stories of prolonged ordeals, loss of wits, speech, motor skills, bowel control—without question Kirk would have been first to agree.) For the others it would be every reason you would guess; some you wouldn't dream of. Leukemia. Bicycle accident. Mysterious falls. But hadn't reality (Ollie wondered aloud to Fran once) always offered this same, crapshoot precariousness? Wasn't it only that their awarenesses, with age, had opened wider to the facts?

No, Fran had answered quietly, staring past the beer in her hand. We're closer to it now, is all.

•

Warming up: doffs the jacket, ties it around his middle.

He should visit her more. But their lives have done that thing most lives do, floated into other habits. She pesters him electronically all the time. Sends reviews, articles, tart little messages. She sees, she's told him, a few nice friends—she actually used the word *nice,* which he takes as ironic; also her way of trying to soothe his concern. She rents movies, enjoys her reading, her gym sessions. Their lives don't intersect unless forced to, which involves a load of driving. Also, he dislikes spending the night away from his own place.

There is no animosity. It's one more vague should-do, on the list of them.

A sigh, joggled by footfalls.

Not many friends left.

Just a fact. They've died, or drifted. People wrote back for a while, until they didn't. You'd suppose Internet life would make it easier, but it seldom worked that way. Online social networks amounted, for him, to a totem pole of faces the size of postage stamps uttering brief, forgettable quips, like the stuff people write when they autograph someone's plaster cast.

People just melted into a different scrim, out there in the clamor.

•

Ollie hears his own sigh. Oxygen deficient, no doubt. Tries to remember to inhale more deeply, fill his lungs with cool, eucalyptus air. No one remembers to breathe. A clutch of skeletal bicyclists zips past so fast he startles—a sound like a slicing propeller. By the time he focuses they're retreating down the road hunched in tight formation, narrow asses rising and falling in unison, buzzing of tires fading with them, leaving him again to the sound of his boots on asphalt, soft dirt. He sees the white roof of the conservatory at some distance, between draping elephant ears, treetrunks.

He wishes he could be more like Fran, articulating thoughts like whipcracks: you often felt, talking to her, as though you'd stepped into alpine air. But Fran's intensity also annoys him. It's unilateral, one-size-fits-all. Kirk used to say to her, in what must have long served as code between them, *Snap out of it.* She's become much quieter since Kirk died. But often when she speaks, he still feels as if something were bearing down on her. At times she seems to vibrate. It took him years to comprehend that this *oh-my-ears-and-whiskers* manner was built into her—its origins lost, as with so much else after we're no longer young, to the vagaries of the past. Now of course it's clearer to him: after a certain age one's history, however shocking, goes transparent, irrelevant. That's the way of it—that's how the culture rolls, as Fran says. You have to shout to be heard.

Fran wrote a weekly column for the county's paper of record—a series of first-person essays. She also reviewed books for it. She's retired from the paper now, but people still approach her at the market or the gym with questioning smiles, telling her they miss the column, urging her to review some new title, offering suggestions and gossip. The column was called Our Town, but her editors had allowed her great freedom with the form; her pieces often amounted to little meditations prompted by local detail—the flock of wild turkeys sprinting across the road single-file one autumn afternoon, for instance, in a calamitous, frantic, cartoon-like chain. Or the year-round vigil of the kerchiefed old lady in the drugstore parking lot, who sleeps all day in a folding chair beside a hand-lettered sign selling keychains.

After Kirk died, Fran asked the paper for an early retirement. Ollie had been sorry she'd done that. He'd thought the column and reviewing might prove extra-helpful to her just then—if not as catharsis, then to lend a bit of focus. But whenever he ventured this idea she'd explain, with patient sadness, that such writing no longer mattered to her the way it once had. She'd had done with journalism, she told him. It only made noise, she said, the way beer makes foam. Besides, she said, journalism was trying to reinvent itself every second in electronic form, worried to death (she'd make a sour face) about *protecting content.* And whatever she poured into a column's space, she reminded him, however brilliant, would evaporate in moments.

Fran still loves reading, though. Meat and drink, she calls it. Watches other people's reviews; e-mails them to him, sometimes with her own commentary (*arrogant idiot* or *I'd read his grocery lists*). Surrounds herself with books—piles of marked up reviewers' copies, newer titles mostly from the library now. Whenever he visits he glimpses the stacks beside her bed, along the floor, coffee table, dining table, even the kitchen counter. Words still weigh in with Fran like gold dubloons—like heavy, glowing pucks. He can envision her biting down on them in mind as if between her teeth, to test their authenticity. If Ollie happens to use a word she likes—maybe a word like feckless— she stops him to tell him so. *Good one,* she'll say, shading her eyes as she gazes, reappraising him with curiosity. (This flusters him—part of him pleased, part of him angry to feel like a child.) She calls the dull city paper from which she retired a sleeping aid, in the same bright tones she used to call her husband a pleasure pig. Ollie's told himself he should be able to own more of Fran's sangfroid. She's only four years younger than him.

He can't. With his toddlers, he never had trouble. They presented as exactly what they were. No submerged mysteries, no punishments. But when he opens his mouth among adults his original purpose snags; words vanish, even if they've been howling in his head. When he opens his mouth among adults the words are swallowed by some deeper hesitation, strong as sleep or hunger: an instinct not to disturb, cause no harm. In result, he knows he appears anxious, watery. An *old woman*. (That is what Kirk called Peter Taylor when he met Fran.) It hadn't helped to grow up in Petaluma—turn-of-the-century farm town, everyone's favorite joke until recently. Though it spreads many miles (ice-cream-colored developments with fake towers and tiles, names like Tosca and Portofino) and though it now boasts a lovely downtown, trendy restaurants, historic neighborhoods lined with sweet old Victorians, its products for decades (until the real estate explosion) remained poultry and dairy. The town still throws an annual egg-and-butter festival; its parade features pretty girls (Cutest Chick competition), livestock, and shiny, customized 1950s pickup trucks.

He spots a red Hacky Sack ball. Kicks it, watches it spin away.

The only child of a librarian and an entomologist, both lifers with the university down the freeway, Ollie is now older than he remembers his parents to be. The house he grew up in smelled of dust, tapioca, tomato juice, gin and tonics (before dinner each evening) and the nostril-pinching chemicals his father used for specimens. Ollie had made sure never to be around for the extinguishing of the butterflies, moths, iridescent beetles—but he couldn't escape the displays. Case after case of them, framed glass mountings covering his father's office walls. While he'd always understood that the specimens were invaluable, that they represented tremendous knowledge as well as beauty, the displays saddened and oppressed him—but like most children with no access to a different opinion, he'd supposed these feelings evidence of his own lack. His job as a child had been to obey and agree, set the table, take out trash, practice piano, do home-work, clean his room. He didn't like sports. He loved the old town's library—loved its smell, which came to stand in his mind for safety—spent a lot of time there. He walked to school alone and walked home alone, concentrating on the tiny wrinkles in the sidewalk beneath him, counting the seams marking each square of cement, pretending to be immersed in that errand when he passed groups of kids, pretending not to hear the low jeers, followed by giggles, that sometimes echoed back from them. A childhood of ghosting your way through.

They died within weeks of each other, his parents, just quietly dried up and stopped, like the apple tree out back that simply ceased living one summer. He was in his thirties then. They left him the house, which he sold—foolishly, some said, after the town became a pricey commuter bedroom—and with the pro-ceeds bought a three-and-a-half-room flat in the Sunset district of San Francisco. (He'd decided against the Castro because it struck him as a quarantined zone and also a zoo; in those years tourists streamed through to gawk and snap photos, for which many of the neighborhood's regulars were only too glad to per-form.) The half room was just big enough for a low bed and tall bookcase—Fran gave him a cartonful, and there were marvel-ous used-books outlets along Ninth and on Judah—he needed only to roll over and reach up for the next title, and it pleased him almost unreasonably that he could examine all his titles while lying on his back.

During the first months, he'd walked Irving Street with a slow, wild happiness, breathing cold sea air: if the day was clear he could glimpse the silver-gray triangle at the west end that was the ocean. His unit was one of a foursquare set, the building like a large shoebox, two blocks from the park. What rankles him now is that everyone in the city, exempting himself and a few others, looks about thirty. As if by unspoken law anyone older's been banished. Like sneaky science fiction: walk around and see thirty-somethings *partout,* pushing barrowfuls of babies, loosening ties, running in packs, laughing in the hip Asian cafés or Irish sports bars, or on the steps of the museums and concert halls downtown. And the clear impression these beautiful kids give, as you watch them, is that they are absolutely certain they've stumbled (by some secret combination of elements unknown even to them but likely involving purity of heart, beauty, wit, and so on)—into this Brigadoon, which manifested moments ago expressly so that they could set foot upon its gentle streets and hills and grass and harbor, make jubilant, expressive little nests along its avenues, strike up love affairs, ingest drugs and booze and overpriced food, have abortions or families, trot around to movies, cocktails, gourmet coffee. It exists only for them. In their faces he reads this: the entire city belongs to them. There is no past. A bunch of stuff happened earlier, troubling, but no matter—there is only the recent past, designed to give over to them. There is no future exempting whatever tasty gifts wait for them behind the fog curtain like guest celebrities, in days and months to come. Ollie is perfectly aware he *was* these people for a good long while, longer perhaps than he may have had any right to. But now their indifference depresses him: also it stings, like a slap. An android breed with infrared vision, the young register only themselves. It makes his physical presence among them—at his favorite bookstores, his burrito or noodle shack—feel ancient and nullified, a dusty can of vegetables on a back shelf.

•

He looks up: blue hole prevailing, taking over.

Of course he still loves his neighborhood.

Loves his little box of a home, his books, his music—his Copland, Respighi, Grieg; his jazz. The marble mortar and pestle for grinding pepper that Ennis gave him (probably stolen), on the wooden table in the kitchen. The yellow chair like the one in Van Gogh's painting of his room in Arles. The view from his kitchen of the library's Spanish tile and other rooftops, pigeon shit–speckled through dirty glass. He'll probably die here. Occasionally he lets himself wonder who will find him—how long that might take—before stuffing the thought away like an old cleaning rag. He knows he should choose some neighbor or acquaintance he can ask to knock every week to make sure he's alive. But he tells himself it's still early for that, and anyway he can't think of who—or even how to ask. He doesn't know the names of anyone on his street, though he knows a few faces. It's one of the things he loves best about the place: locals recognize each other, nod, leave one another in peace. He has often joked about his three-room confines. All that's left for him to do, he's said, is to cut holes in the roof.

The days follow one another. At first slowly, now faster. He cannot account for it. He has more time now than he did when he worked. Much more. Why shouldn't the days feel slower, more spacious? And yet it feels to him as though the clock spins fast-forward, the way they do in cheesy movies.

•

A firetruck wails in the avenues. He stops to plant his feet; twists in both directions, holding his arms the way he would to work a hula hoop, making sure to suck in his stomach: effects a small, relieving *pop* in the chain of bone at his lower back.

He can picture the spinal arrangement. Porous, quick, compliant. Bundled ganglia. Mysterious fluids funneling. *Please: last long.*

Walks on.

•

The quality of the prior night's rest now appears to govern everything. A ritual cramped and hopeful as any distant tribe's: every night he reaches to switch off the reading light (a smallish globe smelling of hot dust as it warms; he worries about locating a replacement when it burns out), arranges himself beneath the bedclothes in his favorite position—curled on his side, a fat pillow folded between his thighs to stack his hips so as to ease his back. Then the small panic slips into his chest.

Like a fish.

He stills himself each time, to pay attention: the cold thing loose and racing behind his ribs, panic he cannot identify. In earlier years he could trace most anxiety to something that had happened earlier, something he or someone else said or did. But this ricocheting thing, a frantic Tinkerbell, has no obvious source, or none he can pinpoint. He waits, feeling its frightened rounds in his chest, until after long minutes it dissipates, absorbed back into his inner walls like a stain. He waits another beat—*what can it mean?*—and finally gives up, pushing his face into his pillow, pulling the covers up to his ears—ears stuffed with silicone earplugs; black velvet sleeping mask positioned over his eyes.

Tries a number of exercises to empty his mind.

Tries breathing in, letting different body parts become heavier with each exhale.

Tells himself *Let it go. Let it all go.*

And often this is just when a host of linked concerns begins parading past his mind's gaze—comic if you discounted the longing for sleep, the mounting anxiousness—each goblin looped to its predecessor like the tail-to-snout smiling pink elephants in Disney cartoons.

Why do things hold together during the night, still there as they were before, in the morning? Buildings. Furniture. Objects. Laws of gravity. Travel reservations. Names. Languages. Agreements. Purchases. Ideas of moral order. Relationships. Streets. While we dream—belief floating like wisps of low-lying fog—why do all these givens hold? Why doesn't the night just drift them away somewhere, like half-filled balloons?

Where do the birds sleep during the night, and especially, during storms? He has never seen them do it (except ducks and geese and egrets at the park, forming a lovely treble clef on one leg, head disappeared under wing). Never seen evidence of their hiding and sleeping places. No one speaks of this. No one seems to wonder about it. He's never seen a film or documentary show it. Like the Stevenson poem about the wind. Who's seen it? *"Neither I nor you . . . But when the trees bow down their heads"—*

Where is Ennis now? Where is Kirk? Nowhere, he answers himself firmly each time. But they live in your mind, and that is why you dream about them.

Is the refrigerator at the right setting of coldness? He adjusted it recently, a modest notch on the dial. Will that hike his utility bill? He's living on carefully parsed installments of the trust his parents left him, together with a stipend from Social Security. The truth is that he is more than comfortable. He spends little; his savings are plentiful. He knows it's irrational to worry about any blip in expenses. In his mind, though, some shapeless calamity lurks off-stage like a distant tidal wave. When it rushes at him he must be fortified, ready to stave it. And he can't abide a tepid refrigerator. Something ghastly about it, too phlegmatic even for him. And of course it would encourage bacteria.

Why did I buy those nectarines out of season? And then throw away the receipt, so there would be no hope for a refund when they turned out, cut open, to be dry and stringy and tasteless?

They must have been flown in from Chile. Ecologically wrong. Probably filled with pesticides. Just as well to toss them. Of course it gave someone a job to provide them, but—

What is causing the gas I am passing? Usually he could pinpoint it if he thought enough about it; often the aroma was hint enough. Ah. Broccoli. Mostly uncooked, for retention of vitamins. Maybe he should cook it more—at least use more of that brownish tincture called Beano. Seems to help, if he can only remember to dose his cabbage and beans beforehand. Yet when he did shake the droplets of tincture over his plate, an uneasiness crept through him—fairy tales? Shakespeare?—that he was dashing poison onto the food. Must remember to research what Beano is made of.

The bright garden of flowers looms ahead, the white apparition.

Another phenomenon's been molesting his sleep lately. He wakes in the middle of the night needing to urinate. Once per night is not bad, for a man his age. (Various men, he has noticed, seem enslaved by the urge, ducking into bathrooms every twenty minutes.) Still, it's *pénible*—a nuisance. He will not let himself look at the clock when he rises—for this reason he deliberately keeps an old travel clock without an illuminated face—though he can tell by the windowlight, with discouraging accuracy, what the hour probably is. He makes his way to the toilet and back to the bed. At that hour the room seems alien, an unknown version of itself, immersed in an atmosphere that has sneaked in and murdered the familiar one.

The alien room's not black nor gray—more a murk. Familiar objects look grainy: he wouldn't be surprised, should he reach out to touch them, if they felt mealy, if their edges crumbled and gave way. (He tries not to touch anything on his way back to bed except the bed itself.) Everything stands as he left it, windows open an inch, distant fanlike whir of the sleeping city. But the stillness feels dense. He can't push away a sense that the world he knows has somehow inverted, sunk to the bottom of an interplanetary sea—that it does this every night; that other laws apply during these undersea hours that he cannot understand. All the cheery appurtenances of daylight, all human history, may have been a dream. He slips back under the still-warm covers and presses his eye mask close and hunkers his body into its favorite curl so he might resume the delicious downward drift, scraps of which still swirl through his arms and legs and torso. But too often his mind has sparked awake and begins to rev, spinning in sand without traction. He tosses and yawns. Tosses and yawns, tosses and yawns until the tears stream, and he must reach under the mask to wipe them away. He can't suppress a mental spasm that wants to solve everything, though there is obviously no solving to be found. He frets during those phantom hours—he's confessed it to Fran—about everything that ever happened since the beginning of time. Including (his face heats to admit) the beginning of time itself. Where are the limits of time, of the universe? How can we go about our lives, alongside the staggering awareness of not knowing?

When he told her this, some years back, they'd been sitting after dinner in the plastic Andirondack chairs on the Fergusons' front porch—a structure so old it seemed to sag in the middle—their feet propped on the low wall fronting it. Early summer evening, ink blue, crickets caroling in full fearlessness, a loud, brazen chorus arriving and subsiding in rounds. Kirk was busy in the house fetching more wine, and a fresh beer for Fran.

After his confession, Fran had given Ollie a look that seemed to open concentrically like a periscope lens.

For fuck's sake, Ollie, she'd said at last. Isn't the time on earth hard enough? Do you have to take on so much extra-credit homework?

•

Even thinking about these questions in the dark—reliable as a jack-in-the box they *boing* forth, leering at him—his face muscles always lock into that same unctuous smile he longs to be rid of. A butler's smile, a rictus. A smile for strangers in the supermarket, dropped the instant they pass. He can blame no one for despising it, though no one's said so. Some nights he digs his fists into the tops of his cheeks, rewarded by a brief relief in the muscles. But he has never, that he can recall, felt unfettered, at perfect ease in his face, his body. Long ago, maybe, in Ennis's arms, in the Forestville cabin. But that was only, in truth, when Ennis was asleep. Latterly, Ollie's had some peace in the bathtub, if the hot water lasts. Also at Fran's, but more so when Kirk was alive. Alcohol helped. Not torrents, but a genial flow.

And now whenever a certain type of man passes his sight-lines—as many do this gentle afternoon in the park, jade leaves sifting and turning, the soft, compacted dirt on the paths fluffing under runners' feet, sun pearling—an ache squeezes his sternum. And he tries, without attracting notice, to look a bit longer. Like the heart-spearing jazz ballad: *"This is all I ask."* Each beautiful man like a riddle, gliding along shooting-gallery style, gliding away before he's had time to absorb it. Solve it.

"Children everywhere, when you shoot at bad men, shoot at me . . ."

He never wants to embarrass anyone. If he could just keep the lovely being in sight, stare deeply enough, he might unlock an answer.

He studies his booted feet. Better if he could *amble*. Nobody ambles, except crazies and drunks. His own movement, he knows, looks more like stalking—the original sense.

Things want solving. Yes.

But for what sort of answer? And how would that work? He slots his palms into his armpits as he lopes.

What if the answer could break open before one's eyes, like a computer screen icon. A concentrated thought would click on the troubling image, the body suddenly explode—cleanly, of course—into a new shape, say a fortune cookie's little rectangle of paper. Then—oh, delightful—if people looked at one another hard enough, intensely enough, the air would become snowy with twirling white fortunes like cherry blossoms.

Too early for real cherry blossoms yet. Coming, though. Six weeks, he gives them.

His gaze roves the meadow next to the garden, its grass close-clipped: three or four toddlers stagger around, giddy in the enormous space, arms floating up like little drunks. Young mothers stand beside the waiting strollers balancing juice bottles, bags of crackers, diapers. Their tired, patient faces. It's how he must have looked all those years during yard duty, watching his pudgy charges as they ran and shouted and collided, oblivious to heat or cold. One would bang into another, fall, wail, and Ollie would move quickly with the sterile wipes, ointment, Band-Aids, gentling words. How heavily the tears poured over peachlike cheeks; how raw the suffering—no matter how many times he went through it, it always amazed him—and how abruptly, with some least distraction, it would halt! Fat oily tears evaporating as if by magic, and not a snippet's memory left on the cheek or in the child of the tragedy he'd just screamed through.

He'd entered the child care world when he'd volunteered for it at the local gym—*health club* the official, lofty term—which drew a moneyed and educated clientele. He'd commenced the work in exchange for membership, since dues were steep. Men who were good with preschoolers showed up rarely—and of course were suspect; parental nerves rasped by horrible media. The staff watched him hard during his trial period, impressed that no matter the quiet young man was so tall—he'd plop down cross-legged on the floor and lift his charges onto a small stool so they could be face to face with him when they talked. The Talking Stool, it was called. Hup! Onto the Talking Stool with you! The kids loved Ollie without hesitation. His height didn't frighten them. They stared into his eyes, which reminded them of their best pale-blue clearie marbles, and wondered at his voice, uncommonly soft. They loved saying his name, or trying to say it, calling to him all day. Ahrry! Ahrry, *watch*. He churned out streams of ideas. They made puppets, put on shows. Organized musical parades, with Ollie playing his alto recorder at the lead (straight out of *The Family of Man*, Fran cracked). Decorated the room, its fenced outdoor yard, for each holiday and season: pumpkins, valentines. Built trains with chairs. Held miniature picnics, spreading old blankets on the ground. Colored, drew, sculpted, sang. Glued glitter. Papier-mâché, clay, fingerpaints, messes be damned. They burst a piñata, and scrambled for the hail of (healthful) sweets. One year he had them paint masks for themselves on paper grocery bags cut with eyeholes, which they wore in the play yard awhile. One little boy became frightened inside the bag and started to cry: was he still himself in there?

Ollie read to them. Babar, E. B. White, all his favorite old titles as well as newer, recommended ones (librarians in the children's section knew him by name and he remembered theirs; their faces lit when he showed up). He led his kids in exercises, dancing. Prepared snacks. Cleaned up with care, handling minor emergencies with swiftness and dignity. And for parents or managers who glanced through the high windows, the sight of a small being floating along on the tall fellow's shoulders while ragtag herds of others clung to his calves, became routine. During that period he completed his teaching credential, and eventually, through one of the gym's grateful parents, found the plummy spot with the Cole Valley school. Twenty-five years at the place had yielded such a legion of fans—a fresh crop every year—he could not easily walk around the city during the day without someone looking twice and racing to catch him: Mr. Gaffney! Mr. Gaffney! Remember me?

Almost there. A good thing. He's tiring.

·

You could argue he'd had thousands of children.

So in a way it hadn't really mattered that he was a lifelong bachelor. Melancholic. Or that he'd loved men. No one ever asked about his love life, or lack of it. Staff parties anywhere in San Francisco resembled (someone once joked) the Star Wars bar, and the city, notoriously, made ample room for oddness. You could say he'd been extremely lucky in many more ways than one: a place to belong. His private life his own. His health intact, against catastrophic odds.

You could say that.

He turns for a backward look at the meadow. Wild lilies line its rim, volunteers. Bundles of fleshy stems shoot straight up like organ pipes, crowned by deep white cups. The lilies always impress him. You can chop them back to nothing and they'll bound right up again. Older blooms wither to translucent tissue, butterscotch-colored, accordion, then disintegrate. A perfect, speeded-up analogy. But too simple. Flowers aren't—unless you believe the Findhorn people—such a festering clutch of rue as humans. Though he sometimes imagines the plants thinking the way he does. He knows they love being watered, left in peace, given sun. That much they manage to make clear. He remembers patting new soil into the bougainvillea up at Fran's (where it's warm enough to keep one year-round, if he helps her haul the giant plant onto the porch just before first frost)— shaking in an extra layer of fertilizer. And the next day every single one of its cascading scarlet blooms—fuschia, in effect; brilliant—every bloom had given birth to a tiny white star, sprung from each bloom's heart at the end of a long delicate white stem like a secret message bouncing forth to greet him. Sometimes two stars per bloom. The plant's body exploding with them, a lacy battalion. He'd wanted to kiss them.

He gropes around in the jacket pocket, now hanging from his waist, for the single cigarette. Glances in both directions. Fran would give him such grief. He lights up, inhales with guilt and relief. Exhales to his side; smoke hovers, vanishes.

He slows a little. Why can't he amble?

Ambling has no destination, that's why.

Perhaps we're more like dogs after all. Fran's chihuahuas. Runty, hairless, trembling. The kind some women carry in a purse or pocket: snouts bobbing out, eyes leaking with inbred madness.

Others of us, larger. Longer fur.

He likes men large. Of course it's been too long to use the present tense. It used to be difficult to find large men: he's horribly tall himself. But bearlike was good. With hair. Not too much, though, and not over the back. The warmth of skin, damp skin. Long gone. Unless by accident, say, he passes someone in the street; he can smell them. His nostrils still keen for it: clean sweat. He'd liked the feeling of being overpowered, thrown about, though he knew that held danger and in fact had never cared for pain. He'd sometimes wished it had been otherwise; that might have made it easier. Fran has lectured him, of course. As if he knew nothing at all. Was there anything Fran did not tell him how to do? *En tout cas* she needn't have: those sorts of risks long past. Luck, purest dumb luck, that he'd escaped the plague.

Takes a last drag, pitches the cigarette. Eyes the smoldering butt, bends to snatch it back, stubs it against the curb til it's cold, tucks it into the jacket pocket. Joggers pass, lips pooched out, steady bursts of air like Lamaze birth practitioners, all grim concentration.

I am sixty-two years old.

•

A good thing, *enfin,* that people cannot hear thoughts. They can guess them, of course. The face betrays them. Experimentally he lets go of the muscles in his cheeks, temples, mouth. Eyelids, scalp. As he marches, he tries wiggling his ears. Someone watching hard that moment might discern the faint movement, so little hair disguises the area. When he was small his father had entertained him that way, wiggling his ears—one of the few tricks his father'd been able to offer. Amazing how some particulars carry. The cotton shirt (white undershirt beneath) tucked into ballooning pants, narrow belt. The bland face, relieved of its spectacles, reminiscent of Babar's—so solemn as the ears, like fleshy flags (a feature Ollie had inherited) slid up and down. Ollie could see the daylight through his father's ears: orange-pink, with tiny veins filtering through.

Ollie keeps his own head shaved now. More a sheen, than hair. It feels clean, but he wishes his skull weren't so—egglike. Some men looked powerful without hair. His baldness, he believes, is unsavory. An institutional nakedness about it, hinting at illness or incarceration. With his alarmed, straight-ahead focus, his driver's license photo resembles a mug shot.

He puffs air into his cheeks so they bulb out. Shakes his face. How loose it feels. Just one of the insults, the myriad insults.

Once, quite by accident, he'd looked straight down into a mirror placed flat on a table. There his face flesh hung, eyes sunken in fleshfolds, sight from a horror film.

The Man with the Falling-Off Face.

•

Crunching along—eucalyptus acorns, strips of bark.

His long feet follow one another toward the spread apron of lawn and garden. His jeans are heavy and dark: he's just bought them at Costco. They fit him the way new jeans fit people in the 1950s, stiff, high-waisted, cuffed at the ankles. He inspects the sidewalk leading to the white structure. Someone has made colored chalk stencils: a perfect stegosaurus in chartreuse, a series of sunflowers. Also a hopscotch grid, now smeared. Past him stream the bicyclists, kite-flyers, laughing dogs.

Here are some of the comments his ears catch, like phrases of music, as couples and groups pass in both directions:

If you dress like that, who's going to protect you?

Rhododendrons are okay, in their place.

In this county if you want to bury someone in your yard, you need a permit.

Those were the days when they gave you an enema before you had a baby.

He loves this park, people at play, ocean air. A heady knowledge sparks it, passed among the others like a weightless beachball, amusement in their eyes. A wide-swinging democracy. (This offsets the fact of everyone being thirty.) He loves catching backdrafts of aftershaves and colognes, cigars, shampoo, hot dogs, marijuana. Though beneath his exuberance, inside his sternum, something wiggles: the little silver fish of night panic.

Ollie tries again to fill his lungs. The morning had begun agreeably as any, with good black coffee and online perusals.

Social networks, news, arts headlines. Very occasionally, porn. Timewasters—but time is his now and he strives to savor this, wrap it around himself like mink. He begins with the online obituaries, skimming past the long job descriptions, zeroing in on the ages, the causes. *Inventor of Chain Link Fence is Dead at 90. First Welcome Wagon Hostess Dies at 87.* Marveling, as always: how democratic the selection. Nowadays any death below the age of eighty—dear heaven, eighty used to mean mummified—he clicks these open at once, eyes racing along, swift and practiced, to the beginning of the second paragraph, where the obit writers place the cause—if they know it. He can almost predict those causes now, mindful of the deceased's age and a few telling particulars. He's been toying for some time with the idea of keeping a secret record of this data, perhaps over the course of a year, then tabulating it into a sort of morbid algorithm—but he cancels the thought each time, worried the preoccupation may start to contaminate his thinking. Besides, they have insurance actuarial types who've already accomplished that—ghastly purpose. They bet on those odds. (Surely they are paid too much for it, too. When the actuarials die, Ollie thinks, if there is a hell, they'll be among the first automatically routed there.) Certain groups—musicians, artists, television and film celebrities, *arrivistes, enfants terribles,* wealthy socialites or their wrecked children—these ended in predictable ways: he rarely dwelt upon them. With men above fifty the culprit, by far most often, was the heart. Here again, though, even youthful photos often suggested the deceased had not lived wisely; in a glance one could see—perhaps even have warned the poor fellow—that it was coming. Founder of the greasy Italian restaurant chain. Inventor of the syrup that froze as it coated ice cream. Long-distance runner who trained midday in the Nevada desert in high summer.

Accidents took their share: planes, boats, cars. (He tries with all his power not to let his imagination re-enact these.) A sprinkling of murders, disappearances. Various cancers or autoimmune diseases, some common, some rare, always lurked as close seconds and thirds; a number of illnesses so exotic they seemed to have dropped from the sky. No sense in it, no reason. The men and women who'd succumbed looked at him from their photographs clear-eyed and vital. He looks a long time at these photographs, trying to make the image come alive again under his gaze—like resuming a stopped film, only now in full color with a sound track, the man or woman moving and talking, the day's sunlight on trees, kids laughing down the street, dogs barking. And though he hadn't known these people personally, trying to assimilate their sudden gone-ness felt like a punch to his chest. Only a fool could ignore that they had dwelt inside their bodies, moved their bodies, with all the careless confidence of the rest of us. Drank their coffee, brushed their teeth, read their mail, scratched what itched. Impossible to avoid envisioning those smiling beings in their last minutes, drained, haggard, appalled. Perhaps not appalled. Perhaps no time for that. He thought of Ennis, of Kirk.

Then he would frown into the fluorescent screen. He knew that he, like millions of others, would forget within seconds the photos and facts before his eyes—the stories of their only given lives—and click away, re-seize his own familiar desires, his obsessing; whether the geranium on the back stairs had been watered, what to eat for lunch. When his own name, age, job, and address were recited in some half line of small print among the other streaming, soundless lists of public record, it would matter even less.

What most perplexed him were certain stealth-bomb cancers, pancreatic among them. They mowed people down. Of course the atmosphere was permeated with thousands of new toxins.

Every so often, a brain aneurysm. Sometimes melanoma.

•

Automatically his hand lifts to the top of his head, the naked skin warm under his palm. Forgot the damned hat again. He always feels idiotic wearing it: a safari-canvas, olive drab, floppy-brim thing Fran bought him—probably from an ad in the margins of the *New Yorker*, designed for the wealthy on holiday. Those ads show a platinum-haired man wearing the hat, tanned, handsome as George Clooney, squinting out into the distance toward some next hearty adventure. That man could be wearing rabbit ears and still look rugged. When Ollie wears the hat he knows he appears a nerd—missing only the bad case of acne, the Coke-bottle spectacles. Still, the pink patch at the top-rear of his head, a yarmulke-sized clearing, will grow pinker, unprotected. Not good. Melanoma claimed enough of those he tracked in the *Times*—many, in fairness, had worked in deserts—that he felt a constant, watery unease every time he stepped into direct sunlight.

Has he remembered to apply sunscreen? Another spasm: he cannot remember doing it or not doing it. This happens more. Deodorant, vitamins, the daily statin pill. A blank screen pulses in that part of the rewound film where the recollected action should be. He reaches for the view of himself in the mirror running the waxen stick over his armpits, recapping it, opening the lid of the pill jar. Instead, nothing. White fog. Or the film snaps and flaps around the reel, and he's stuck to an image of himself performing the action—with no idea when it happened. Followed, of course, by the pop-up flare of anxiety. Too many instances. Pouring cereal into the coffee-grounds basket one morning. Entering a room at the precise moment of losing the reason he'd gone there. In the same way, the comely idea that had one beat earlier been yattering along in his head like a talk-show host flies away without warning, leaving not one feather of itself behind. He's done some reading. It happened to everyone, but you could fight it. Fran forwards him articles by e-mail. He should exercise, take antioxidants, learn a foreign language—work his brain harder.

Aghh, he says aloud. No one hears. Cars purr past, sound systems thumping.

He rents French films sometimes. They have to be a certain kind—can't be the sort that blindside you with horror—that chop your hands off, as Fran puts it. He assesses this by reading about them carefully beforehand. He loved *May Fools* and *Small Change,* but those were eons ago, Malle dead so many years. He loved *Tous Les Matins du Monde* for the music, though he could have predicted the elder daughter's suicide within the movie's first fifteen minutes. As one ages, certain formulae in film and television telegraph their outcomes so ham-handedly he's wondered whether he was missing some subtler intention. (None arrives.) He hates crosswords and Scrabble, but he does the Jumble puzzle in the newspaper—cheats by jotting combinations of letters on a separate sheet, building tall columns of them until one finally congeals before his eyes. A tiny sparkle races through his brain when that happens, and he is convinced this sparkle must be helpful, though he suspects it does not fulfill the hard-brainwork quota.

As for exercise, of course, he walks. Across the city, bridges, neighborhoods. Early mornings best, a lovely secret time along the streets—except for having to detour around the homeless crumpled in porticoes, over grates, washing themselves in public fountains, urinating against buildings. He walks until his shins ache; goes home to rest his legs on a stack of pillows. When they feel better he goes out and walks some more.

●

Sun has swept all fog aside like a cobwebby veil, and a deep blue vault of sky, blue that promises gold inside itself, holds the park in two arms. Nearing the green pour of lawn fronting the conservatory, he stops at a vendor's wagon. The notion of a warm pretzel has caught him up: yeast and chewiness and salt combine excellently in the mouth with coffee. Also it seems romantic. Proof one's alive. He should confine himself to whole grains, but it is only one pretzel. *I participate in the day. I take part in the joyful human scene.* Smiling, he requests his treat from the young woman waiting behind the display case. Bottles of colored syrup line its front.

That's five dollars, she says as she hands it across the tops of the syrup bottles, smiling back at him in the sun. She is plump, brown-skinned. The small, flat loop of dough is wrapped in thin white paper.

His face empties. The mental soundtrack, until that moment all lilting Vivaldi, sags into goo.

Five dollars?

He repeats the words as though he's been shot by them, unable to control his tone or the alarm in his eyes. He must sound like any of the dozen loonies the young woman surely encounters all day. His face fills with heat—though no one else stands near, thank heaven.

When did they start costing five dollars? he murmurs, trying for a humorous tone that might partly erase his shock, feeling only more ridiculous as he says it. No sense pretending he has not lived here thirty years, or that he never asked for a pretzel in all that time. In truth he cannot remember buying a pretzel here, or anywhere. He's lost track of their prices—never kept abreast of them; he's too tight to buy snacks in the park. Yet he can't help his indignation; it seems insane to charge that much money for the thing in his hand, which in no way resembles (a child's memory?) the outsized, fat, doughy treat he anticipated. The pretzel in his palm is the size of a small, flat cookie.

Five dollars buys an entire loaf of bread. Good, sprouted multigrain. Or used to. He doesn't say this. His heart, for some reason, is pounding. He searches his wallet, desperate to avoid lingering another minute over the breaking of a larger bill. With inexpressible relief, he finds five singles. The air around him has grown still. The young vendor waits silently, her restraint something he recognizes, his heart tightening—restraint he himself has practiced ten thousand times in the presence of louts and the deranged: meticulous calm lacquering over private amusement. He cannot bear being dumped, in her mind or anyone's, into that teeming pile: the mad, the marginal, the lost. He hastens off into the bright day, his vision black, and devours the pretzel in three bites.

He longs to eat a roomful of them.

•

He has forgotten to get coffee. Just as well. Too late in the day for it; sleep would be mauled. But now he is thirsty from the pretzel's salt. The afternoon's grown inexplicably hot, pressing down. His skin is clammy; his heart only beginning to calm. He finds a drinking fountain, takes a seat on the concrete steps leading up to the majestic horticulture conservatory: a Taj Mahal–like vision snowy against the saturated sky, renovated some years ago after a storm blew the last one down. He's never seen the renovated interior; he should go in and have a look. It might cheer him. He loves plants and trees—also, he tells himself, it's a wholesome a mission, a palpable project. Projects are good. Rising, knees cracking, he heads for the conservatory entrance—but at the front of the roped walkway a sign is posted:

Closed after 4:00 p.m.

He checks his watch. Exactly four. His eyes smart, and he feels a ludicrous urge to weep. Blood sugar must be low, pretzel notwithstanding. Of course the accursed thing hadn't been big enough to feed a finch. He stands unsteadily a moment, then returns to the concrete stairs and lowers the unpadded bones of his ass to the stone surface, his long knees angled up. Couples are seated at different distances from him, scattered along the wide, shallow steps, laughing and kissing. Between and among them, families trudge up and down laden with cameras, ice cream cones, maps, howling babies. The lawn and blooms— tulips?—spread before Ollie in lurid diamond patterns, green, orange, white, red. He squints at the banks of flowers. Too bright. They don't look real, though they must be. The people around him, busy with themselves and each other, ignore him.

Of a sudden he's overcome by a wash of haplessness, by his own total irrelevance—sees no longer the garish flowers in their geometric patterns but instead the shaded water under the ole-anders in his parents' backyard, where he sat for countless sum-mers admiring the baby frogs testing their new legs, in perfect tender miniature frogness. He sees his hands wrapped around the red mug of Ovaltine, which he drank constantly at the butter-colored formica table—like cocoa but with a puzzling vitaminish aftertaste—to save labels for a decoder ring, which when it finally arrived spelled out the disappointing message: *Drink Ovaltine.* His mind whiffs the smell of charcoal lighter fluid, the fatty, carbon-flavored juice and bright sting of mustard with the first bite of hot dog, his mother's green-and-white-checked skirt scented by Pond's cold cream, where he'd bury his shy face when strangers spoke to him. He'd loved to wrap himself, in the yard, inside the sheets she pinned to the clothesline; stiff, smelling of sun and wind.

This gave way to another remembered scent, black Bakelite of the rotary-dial phone, a strange, chewy, synthetic pong. And next to the phone sat the parakeet's cage: blue-and-yellow Lily, chittering and burbling, dancing side to side: the belled mirror she pecked at, the branch of millet seeds, the piece of white hard stuff fastened to the cage with a bit of wire: was it called whalebone? His mother had told him birds liked to sharpen their beaks against it the way you'd strop a knife, though he'd never seen Lily do it. His mind glides around the house like a ghost's Steadicam, zooming in and out: the gilt book-spine titles (*Two Years Before the Mast, David Copperfield, The Way of All Flesh*). Jars in the cupboard: Jif peanut butter, Mary Ellen jam, boysenberry. Oblong cans of sardines showing a fisherman in yellow sou'wester on his boat's deck. No limit—on days when he'd slept well the night before—to what he could conjure in perfect, full-color clarity. The tarnished pewter frame of the mirror in the hall, fluted around the rim. Dusty vents of the wall heater, ticking. The black-and-maroon paisley fabric of the sofa. The rust-colored mineral stain under the water spigot in the bathroom sink.

His greatest longing was to find again the Rouault painting that hung in the living room—he had never been able to locate it again, no matter how he scoured the online catalogs. A seated mother, a child at her knee—beside them a laundry basket filled with blue-white clothing, on top of which reposed a small pair of scissors. Chalky blues, blacks, silvers. Mother and child gazed at one another; their features indistinct, but the tenderness between them had filled him with mystery. If he could just find it again, he might be able to decipher it. Certain objects, like the painting, had taken up residence inside him—trying to tell him something. If he could somehow enter them back (he'd believed) they'd unlock the meaning of the adult universe—a shadowy and confusing place where words and actions often meant things you could not guess, or even the opposite of what they seemed. Even now each memory seems to present the same riddle—each urging him to grope around in some invisible pocket of itself, for the hard prize of meaning.

He lowers his head, closes his eyes.

•

Someone touches his arm.

Yo, sir?

He glances up. The young woman bent toward him has stripes of electric blue in her black hair—the dye looks stiff, like paint—the hair itself arranged in a series of eclair-shaped rolls. She can't be fifteen. She is outfitted in black; silver rings lace her nostril, ears, upper lip.

You okay, sir? Do you need anything?

He thanks the girl, touched by the *sir* issuing from black-lined lips. He tries to smile warmly at her. He senses his mouth, in that effort, must resemble a distressed cartoon mouth, all wavy lines.

I'm fine, thank you. I appreciate your asking.

These episodes have happened before—the momentary sense of falling, followed by a series of hyperclear images, memories, smells. He knows they'll come again, perhaps accelerate. It happens to old people, old men.

The barber shop. He'd first grasped that men grew old when his father brought him there, as he watched and listened to them sitting in their chairs, trading complaints in half-swallowed, chalky voices. The scissors went *snick snick;* bits of hair fell to the floor and onto the big white cloth draping the men while they talked. Odors of hair oil and alcohol, jars of clear blue liquid holding black combs, calendars on the wall, the red-white-blue poles outside with their infinite striping—endlessly appearing, disappearing. Where did the stripes come from; where did they go? The barber placed a steaming cloth on the men's faces and let it sit there before he shaved them. (In the bath, he now loves draping a steamed washcloth over his face.) The men had silver bristles sticking out their ears and nostrils; mounded bellies that rode high and round as any pregnant woman's. They wore short-sleeved white shirts and suspenders with metal clips. When Ollie was made to shake their hands he could smell them: camphor (though he did not know that word then), medicinal ointments and liniments, tobacco, bay rum—and something else, a fragile, sickening smell, the smell of fading life. They talked of retail stores or gas stations or burger stands that had once stood at certain spots, now gone. They talked about prices, politicians. Sometimes they barked a laugh but their voices were sour, and the fact that they agreed on anything seemed not to comfort them but to make them more sour. Their words puzzled Ollie. He began to feel that somehow he had caused their problems, that by being born he had colluded with a looming evil, like Godzilla, that meant to harm these old men. But—he kept thinking—*I haven't done anything except get born.* He'd cast about for ways to make his queasiness go away; forced himself to look out the window at creeping traffic or the spinning striped poles, or the calendars. One showed a painting of a partly undressed kneeling lady with hotly rosy cheeks who held the back of her hand to one cheek, alarmed eyes rolling sideways in an *oh-dear* expression. The other calendar showed a photo of a wide street lined with autumn trees, branches thick with leaves of an orange-gold so rich your eyes swam inside it.

The old men would pat him on the head.

And now he's entering their mindstates, their bodies.

Pray heaven he doesn't smell like them. But how can he know? Who'd tell him?

Fran would. He'll ask her.

What shames him now is how remorseless he felt toward the elderly, growing up. Unthinking. Knee-jerk cruel. He'd kept it silent, of course. His own parents were old—older than other parents, because they'd produced him late—but that awareness had not helped his tolerance. The old smelled strange. Their bodies sagged and bloated as if their innards, like a quilt's stuffing, had slid and collected at the bottom. Hair vanished from scalp and grew from nostrils, moles, ears. Skin scaled or crinkled or dessicated to something like paper, blotched with pools of dark color which could in no way be passed off as freckles; blue veins swam beneath the surface or protruded like tubes. Ears stretched long as wattles. Noses spread and drooped; so did breasts, eyelids, testicles, bellies. Gums retracted from teeth and teeth themselves, long as a horse's, cracked and stained brown-yellow so that grins turned ghoulish. Eyes dulled and watered and bore weird markings: sometimes a white band bordered each iris as if threatening to obliterate the color, like a cathode tube losing its picture. Cheekflesh and upper arms sank into jowly purses that shook like unset custard when they moved. And the old moved by inches, blocking his path in stores and intersections as if choreographed in a stunning feat of timing, tormenting him to the point of gasping aloud. Even lately—driving behind someone who crept so slowly as to seem to hover in place, or standing in line at the drugstore—the coupons, the intricate needs, excruciating refund processes—a line so paralyzed even the air around it has stopped—he feels his rage well up like lava. *What good are you anymore?* he wants to scream at them. *Why bother?*

Do people think this way about him now?

The woman selling pretzels today, possibly. If she gave him a thought at all.

•

Late afternoon sky a cobalt dome, seamless, depthless. The water at the Marina, covered with windsurfers and catamarans, will be reflecting that color right now.

Light scrubbed. Early spring.

A few living individuals still know his name.

His own long history, otherwise, has vaporized. So over, as people say, it won't even be a dream anyone remembers.

This thinking, whenever he tries to describe it to her, always makes Fran chuckle.

Dear Ollie. Getting yourself all worked up.

He blinks, looks out into the polleny light like a child waked from its nap.

S o run this by me again, honey.

She pours more wine into his goblet, concentrating hard—but part of the stream sprouts sideways like a demon wing, spattering the old table—Christ almighty she cannot ever pour cleanly, ever, any more than she can ever succeed at peeing in a straight line standing up—and she swipes up the purple spatter with a paper napkin. The wine is delicious, heavy with blackberries and pepper. The goblet alone is a wonder, tall-stemmed, thick, blue-green: spiral of silver air bubbles caught forever in sea-colored glass. Window light, framed by rampant leaves, haloes the space. The table beneath the goblet is bare walnut, dark as an old piano and pocked and scarred, but solid—a table she's always loved, that Kirk owned, like most of the rest of their stuff, before she met him. Table where they'd all eaten hundreds of dinners after which, overcome with food and drink, she'd feel her eyelids fall and have to trail away to bed, whereupon she'd hear the ice rattling onto the counter, popped from its plastic mold:

Kirk would lift out the bottles of hard stuff for his glazed guest (often Ollie) and stay up later still, gnawing at the usual chewtoys—politics, the death of art, comparative prices for roofing or paint jobs or tree-trimmers, whatever the men could still admit to. Cigars were often produced. She loathed the habit. Ancient, yes, but so what.

Only when the men's words began to smear, when they'd forgotten what they were saying—none ever admitted to that, either—would they consent to wobble off and pass out, teeth unbrushed, fully clothed, reeking like chemistry sets. She'd throw Kirk into the shower first thing next day. *And please scrub your teeth. And use lots of mouthwash, please.*

Ollie sips his wine, pale eyes out the window, blue irises translucent. Full of guarded longing, as usual. Gathering himself.

She'll wait. She has time.

This still amazes her. Having time.

She runs a thumb and forefinger down the goblet stem. So often she'd marveled, all their years, how unbearable it always seemed to Kirk—to most men—to let the night take over. An unspoken rule, stiffening the air as hours passed: *Don't let the night win.* Of course it was a doomed resolve, a fixed fight every time. She couldn't think of many women who behaved that way—waging silent, cunning battle against the invading night. Women simply went to bed. If they had to swallow an Ambien to halt the internal newscast, that wasn't the grossest sin.

But for the men, that grave whiff of myth about it: give in to sleep and you lost. Biology to consider, too. Caveman imperatives, sentry's vigil. Sleep made you vulnerable, could get you killed. Men seemed wired to refuse it—the takeover of evening—with everything in their power.

Mostly, the weapon of choice was alcohol.

She'd watched it acted out afresh every time, a hundred thousand nights; each as if it had never happened before.

Like a kid's fear of bedtime.

Fran lets her head tilt. Either that, or the more obvious: the Dylan Thomas school of night-resistance. Sleep as death, as the end of pleasure.

The end of pleasure. She feels her brows lift. Nothing nobler nor more complicated.

Her eyes drift to the window where Ollie is gazing, in silvery-green light. Kirk never remembered much about those booze-soaked sessions with his pals. No second thoughts. Sometimes when she asked him (casually, so as not to seem to pry) he remembered a few dull details. The men talked a lot, it seemed, about money. Lost, gained. More caveman duty. Survival check, roll call. Heroic, in its way. Of course he could have been censoring, protecting the cave's privacy. Maybe they spoke of fantasies, of secret hungers to visit hookers, change identities, rob banks, disappear—reappear elsewhere as someone else. Maybe everyone played with that idea once or twice. She smiles vacantly at Ollie, who is taking another pensive sip. No denying: Kirk never regretted one moment of those thousands of celebrations. You could even suggest—exempting sex, exempting history and sports—those sessions were what he'd lived for.

Them, and her. To be technical.

No regret. Not even for nights she'd had to hoist one of his arms over her shoulders to haul him to bed. He would insist (indignant) he could do it himself.

He always turned extra-sweet when he was pasted. Floppy. Which made getting him bedded Frankensteinishly more difficult. Grinning, noodle-loose, spectacles lost somewhere, face and features softened to pudding. You're a hot little mama, he'd murmur into her face as she propped him along, his breath yeasty. You have an adorable little body. I can't believe how tiny your feet are. He'd say this as he glimpsed her brown loafers on the mat by the front door.

Yes, sweetheart, she'd mutter, trying not to trip while stepping alongside. Now let's just get you horizontal.

He insisted on lifting her sweater and kissing each of her breasts before he'd resign himself to sleep. One after the other, beaming at each breast as if he'd reared them.

Her hand tightens around the glass stem. She wraps it with the other.

The house always so still around them. It had no opinions, yet its surfaces forgave. She'd sensed this the moment she first laid eyes upon the house: mounting the wooden steps to the bowed porch, the pink roses big as baseballs, blooming messily. Kirk always chopped the rosebush back to nubs in winter, a fist of stubby knuckles. She's let it spread. She should probably move, sell the house, set up in a newer condo with stark surfaces. But she loves the house.

Difficult to clean, the earth always trying to swallow it. It may also contain a ghost or two. But they feel circumspect. And they aren't Kirk's.

She does talk to Kirk. She talks to the hole-of-not-him, a hole which somehow becomes him, filling the air and space around her. A saturation of him-ness, buzzing in the atoms of things. *You're here, aren't you,* she'd said aloud to the rooms, the first time she felt it. Once in a while she sends him silent bulletins, often in the form of complaint, incredulity larded with curses. As though he were now a committee of one, auditing her follies. She tries to keep it short.

She pours herself another small splash now, sets the bottle aside, resumes her position in window light: cheek against a palm, elbow planted in the other palm. A triangle of inquiry.

Okay then. You were out for a harmless walk and you craved a harmless pretzel? And it all came tumbling down?

•

Ollie looks up. Fran's words so often prick him—they seem to seize his reports and start dancing them between her feet like a soccer ball. As if mocking his earnestness. *Reducing* it. At the same time, her accuracy often smacks him awake. Also, she can be funny.

He does what he usually does: lifts his lips. He's experimented, over years, with responses to Fran. It's less trouble, finally, to admit his own *faiblesses* with her. She won't punish him (though she may bat him around a bit). He really has no one else to tell anymore and she knows that, too: most kindly of all, she never says so.

Often, he lets her yabble on while he dreams of other things. Until this moment he's been remembering his first bicycle. A sparkling silver-and-fuschia Schwinn, except no one would have called it *fuschia* in those days. The magic of learning to ride: a heavenly miracle to be able to fly on two narrow, vertical tires. But then Tommy Blake from down the street had materialized and wanted to try the bike, and Ollie had let him because Tommy had beautiful white-blond curls and milky skin, and one minute into the test-drive Tommy had teetered and shimmied and careened the shiny Schwinn into the curb, scratching and denting its fender, left it where it fell and ran home bawling.

Yes, he says to Fran after a moment. Maybe the whole event only had to do with food. I should have eaten earlier that day, something with more protein. But I felt I was—

Losing it, she says.

Yeah.

He peers at her.

It's about aging, Fran. Getting old.

She cocks her head. Come again?

Fran—listen, I know this will sound insane.

He looks away a moment.

But would you please, please let me know—would you just tell me straight out—if I start to smell old? If I start to smell, you know, that way? Like an old man?

She absorbs this. Then, pointedly:

One: yes, I would. I will. And two: Ollie, of course you know that's ridiculous.

He glances at her, and a weariness flits through him. He dreads her bullying. He has no energy for jousting anymore. Not that he ever did. Yet too often he seems, unwittingly, to invite it.

Is it? he asks.

She leans forward. You're in terrific health, despite all the crap you let worry you. You're a fine-looking man—please don't argue with me; it's true. You're distinguished. And you're free. You have means. You still have your wits. And the world is open to you. Just like a Henry James character. You can make a victory tour. Figure things out. Things can happen for you now, Ollie.

She looks at her hand clasping the blue glass stem, then past it into the middle-distance.

What I mean is, she says, you can make things happen.

He smiles. You sound like a self-help book.

She doesn't smile. I'm serious, Ollie. This is the time when you can do what all those smug-ass people at my gym are always talking about. Live the dream.

At this she does smile, sheepish. She despises those people and they both know it. The *white-wine-and-lean-meat people*, she calls them.

She rises, pushing her chair back abruptly; its legs shriek

against the linoleum. Time for a beer, she says. Right back.

He hears the sucked-apart-rubber of the yanked refrigerator door, the crack-spriss of the opened bottle, the coin-like clatter of the bottlecap hitting the counter. She returns, bottle in hand (refuses to use a glass; claims this spoils the taste) and seats herself with a sigh that sounds like a fluffy pillow being sat on; takes a long pull from the cold brown bottle whose glass is already coated with mist.

She sets the bottle down, sighs with pleasure. Mother's milk, she murmurs. Her wine goblet's still at hand. (Her term for this, *two-fisting*, embarrasses him.)

Oh, wait! She sprints back to the kitchen.

From her sound system, barely audible, he hears Bach, solo piano. Italian Concertos, Alexandre Tharaud. Her latest crush. She goes through phases. For a while it was only Glenn Gould, then Till Fellner. Then nothing but lute and early music, Jordi Savall and so on. Now she's back to Bach, but the artists are not Gould. Ollie has inspected the CD cases, read the liner notes. They're young European men, prodigies, sepulchral beauties, carved and pale. They have wonderful hair, bed hair, French hair. Once in a while she makes Ollie listen, forbidding talk, through the entirety of a piece. He remembers a Lizst phase, the *Consolations*. Also *Un Sospiro*. For a while, she told him, she played that one every day until she began hearing it in her dreams—then in the daytime. The melody ransacked her, she said. When she played passages for him she sat with her hands in her lap, head dropped, dangling redbrown curls. At the opening bars he closed his eyes. The music held a radiance that felt wrought, as if from incalculable pain. It made the skin on his neck prickle in lines, marching up over his scalp. The two sat silently. When the piece finished she lifted her face and said, not looking at him, I want to make something that fine one day.

This bothered him. It seemed exclusionary. He said nothing.

He knows the pieces she's playing now. Each a sibling of the other; each a calm soliloquy. Framed, systematic reasoning. *If this, then this and also this,* so how can it fail to follow that this. A great deliberateness. The sounds enter him at chest level and spread concentrically. Like Vicks VapoRub.

Another old-man memory!

Fran's words have tensed him to defend himself, but the Bach softens him (the wine, too). This is how she operates, he reminds himself.

He hears more refrigerator activity, clanking plates.

Her solitude feels too enforced here, Bach or no. Fran holes up. Doesn't busy herself with whatever he supposes women her age do—though he's not close to many women her age, or many women, or many people at all anymore. He should ask her to describe a typical day—something she's asked him. He's unwilling to turn the question back on her. It seems intrusive, a bit condescending. He can guess how her day unfurls: a little reading, puttering in the house, errands, exercise, the getting of food, perhaps some music, tidying up, maybe a bath, more reading. He recrosses his legs, slings an arm over the chairback. They're probably too alike, he and Fran, and not in good ways. Isn't it interesting, she once mused calmly to him, that neither of us really has any friends? He'd stared at her as if she'd kicked him. And as he cast about for some sort of rebuttal, she was already rabbiting on. My own doing, she was saying. People invite me to dinners as an act of charity. Couples our age. They do it for Kirk, their memory of him. Kirk loved that stuff and I didn't, and everybody knew it. Even though (her eyes went away; she pressed her hands together and dove them between her knees) I made all the required motions. (Her eyes grew hard.) Mailed all those fucking greeting cards. Year after year.

Birthdays, anniversaries, surgeries, hangnails. Kirk had no time for it. Holy *God* how much time did I spend staring at those card racks, matching stupid-ass pictures and words to stupid-ass recipients, like some goofy form of solitaire? Thanking, praising, congratulating, sympathizing. Placing them before Kirk to sign, like a president signing checks. The kicker is, no one was fooled. Everybody saw right through it. Mr. Jolly and his Inscrutable Bitch wife.

Fran made her face moony, mimicking public wonderment in singsong: How can they *be* together? They're so *opposite.* What's up with *that?*

She shrugged. People mean well. That's the prison of it. Everyone means well. We all go through with the dinners once in a while, everyone relieved as hell when it's done. The thing I can never get over is what a screaming dullness rules the room in their midsts, without him. Like a pre-sunk soufflé. Every gathering the same. All of us drowning in good intentions but no one has any ideas, nobody wants to stir things up the way Kirk did. Kirk was oxygen.

Here she'd sigh and look away, and Ollie would try, rather desperately, to bring up some other focus. Never mind the implicit insult to himself, about friendlessness. *Au fond,* she's right. His own friends are distant or dead, or the kind he hails with platitudes and immediately forgets. Those latter sort could die this minute and he wouldn't feel much: he is certain the reverse is also true. It's not personal, of course. You'd disperse all your energy, all your wits otherwise.

He means to ask Fran again about getting a pet. She melts a little every time she meets a dog or cat—he notices when they go walking—and he has read about the good effects on single people, especially aging people, of owning an animal. But he knows that if he asks he'll hear the answer she always gives, the answer he'd give himself if anyone put the question to him. Animals shit and shed and pee and puke, and they cost money. Ignoring them for five minutes feels cruel. Worst, when they die, it bloody kills you.

He unslings his arm from the chairback, takes another sip. One more reason to love the city: never any indictment of those who live alone. (Though heaven knows there seem to be enough dogs there to start a whole new city just for dogs.) In smaller communities, a solitary life is automatically suspect. Fran herself has told him this. People narrow their eyes, try to fix you up, require you to defend, explain.

She returns bearing a shallow clay bowl of olives, purplyblack kalamata and green with red-pepper flakes, fat and oily.

Gotta meet that salt quota, she says, seating herself, selecting one of each kind and popping both into her mouth. They're pitted, she says, pushing the bowl toward him.

Then she frowns. Ollie, are you remembering to eat? Should we go get something real to eat right now?

Fran buys almost all of what she eats in plastic tubs from the deli section, along with rotisserie chicken. She also loves taqueria food, and though she is a small woman, can shovel in a giant plate of it with no discomfort. He's watched her do it.

I'm fine, Fran. I had a big lunch. (This is a lie, but he knows she has nothing to eat, and doesn't want the lather of racing off somewhere.)

She eats two more olives, still frowning. I don't believe you, but okay. So where were we?

Living the dream, he says. He rubs his hands together, sits up straighter, makes his face attentive. What might my life coach recommend?

He watches her mind skim over the planet's surface, alighting, rejecting, zooming on. The Bach, meantime, talks to itself.

And now we see. *That there is this. And we can know. That makes it thus and such and thus.*

At last Fran says: Why not go somewhere, Ollie?

She breathes into her hands, chilled from the beer bottle, and places them between her blue-jeaned knees. Her hands get cold easily, like his. She's wearing a teal-green sweater that makes her short curls redder. She colors it, finally, after years of resisting that. After Kirk's death she developed a stripe of white at the crown of her scalp, at first oblivious of it—then one day the shock of noticing sent her straight to the telephone. The white patch made her look, she said, like Cruella de Vil. *Chestnutty* is the shade she claims she now aims for. Sometimes it comes out darker, most times reddish, really a very pretty reddish. Ollie always praises the result. Lucky to *have* hair, he reminds her. Then they squabble about him growing his out, which she begs him to do. For a while he took pains to explain to her that what hair he has left amounts to a laurel of steel wool: now he just changes the subject.

The world is big, Fran is saying. You love art. You love architecture. You have some money, no ties. Why not? Running away works. At least it's always worked for me.

Her face is curious, friendly. A micro-thin irritation threads her voice, but he also hears her efforts to tamp that below radar. She is thinking about her own past, he knows. A fair amount of running took place in it. (She lit out for the Peace Corps, in West Africa, while he was quaking through college.) But she also seems just now to be casting a line into the murk of his thoughts, willing to wait for a tug. Still, her words pinch him. *No ties.* Code for *no life.* Though he knows she hadn't meant it that way. Or not exactly.

He sighs. He takes a green olive, tastes it. Fabulous: oily garlic, red pepper flakes. She's an olive snob.

Frannie—I flew to Scottsdale last winter for a week. To warm up, wander around. Remember?

She nods. You stayed in a Ramada, and ate in a Mexican place with sawdust on the floor, where they gave you a vibrating gizmo to let you know your table was ready. And an Italian place that played nothing but Dean Martin, where the walls were crowded with photos of gangsters. And you couldn't stay up late enough to hit the clubs—you decided you didn't like the sort of thing the clubs offered anyway. And the people you saw shopping during the day were rich and white and thin, and the women had breast jobs and big hair and zillion-dollar cowboy boots.

He smiles crookedly, shifting his weight on the chair. It pains him to hear his impressions parroted back. They sound snobbish and smug in the retelling. When he'd first confided them to her, he realizes with a pang, he'd thought these descriptions witty.

Yes, yes, all that, he says, waving a hand. But when I flew back to SFO, I couldn't find my car.

He hugs himself, shivered by the memory. Dusk, tired and dispirited, stung as always by the unavoidable moment of stepping into the arriving passengers zone and being greeted by the straggle of hopeful faces, some holding signs: *Julia Corbett* or *Hilton Pipefitters* or *Welcome Esperanza and Raoul*. All the faces register him for less than an instant, then their eyes flick past him. He moves past the faces and hand-lettered signs, trying to arrange his own face and bearing so he telegraphs a bristling *bien-être—I am a happy and well-adjusted individual who knows what he is about*—at the same time dandling in his mind some airbrushed version of re-entering the life of home, knowing the flat will stare at him, cold and mute and stale, that he'll begin striding around dumping junk mail and turning on lights and

machines and appliances—heater, television, even the oven—
just to bring to it a sense of moving blood.

Then, after hastening through the airline's arrival lobby, rid-
ing the long rubber walkway in a windowless cement tube, past
the neon light-sculptures, the ads for medical insurance, to the
multilevel parking garage spreading in all directions, confusing
even in its so-called rebuilt form. Deserted. Soundless. Levels
and areas marked by letters and numbers, none of it making
sense, identical, colorless, signage no help—up and down the
elevator he'd ridden, heart pumping faster and faster, scamper-
ing out onto the asphalt at each floor staring left and right, desperate to spot anything familiar under the anemic milk of fluorescent bulbs—the darkness, the concrete echoing his footsteps,
all such corny signals for pending horror that it might have been
funny had he not been so unnerved. No humans except, briefly,
a dejected-looking woman dragging a wheeled bag toward the
elevators—he couldn't bring himself to address her, frightened
as he was—not even a security guard driving one of those electric carts. He'd tried to calm his pounding heart as up and down
and out into the vast empty dark he stepped again and again,
the elevator dinging witlessly into emptiness at each floor, his
own contorted face gaping back at him in the mirroring brass
of the elevator doors, panting with horror, fully aware his state
was irrational. The incident had so shaken him he could never,
not even now, recall the actual moment of finding the car. He
had driven home trembling. Though he could, of course, have
summoned help—surely he wouldn't have been the first to get
lost here—he'd wondered, that day, whether it was symptomatic.
Whether he was falling apart.

He opens his hands to her. A nightmare, he says softly.

She listens. Never static, her face, and often tricky to read:
what appeared bright affection could camouflage what he'd later

learn (shocked each time) was pitilessness. It struck him that these attitudes coexisted in her, swishing around together but never interpenetrating. Sympathy and scorn, oil and vinegar.

She reaches to pull one of his hands from its tight wrap of folded arms around his chest—she'll see his bitten-down nails, he thinks helplessly, trying to curl his fingers under—and she holds it like a paw in both of hers. Hers are cool, dry. For some reason the gesture reminds him of old movies, when someone tries to revive a fallen comrade by patting his hand. *Speak to me!*

So you feel, Fran is saying evenly, that because you got disoriented in the parking garage, you should not travel? You're incapable of it?

Her words tap his chest with a forefinger. As usual, they contain seeds of compassion and ridicule. He'll ignore the latter: the seed of the former is enough. He's talked to no one for so long—he can't even remember how long. Great balloons of thought billow forward, pushing.

It's more than that, Fran. I have—I can't seem—I have this fear of . . .

He doesn't know how to name it.

Fear of travel? Fran inquires, chewing more olives, licking her fingertips.

He draws a breath.

Fear of a certain kind of travel. If it's domestic, if it's somewhere—established, I guess I mean—biggish towns and such, within the states, it doesn't seem so bad. But remote, or second or third world, even places Americans go all the time— especially isolated places—what happens is—

Ah, I'm not proud of this, he finishes lamely. (Ludicrous, he thinks. Pathetic.)

She frowns, wipes her hands, stands again, this time lifting the chair an inch back as she does, so it doesn't scream.

Let's have some new sounds, she says.

She marches across the room to her boombox; crouches over the shoebox of CDs leafing through them, clacketa clack clack. He sighs. What a youthful body she's kept, he suddenly thinks, watching her. The knobs of her spine make a rounded, raised track in the center of bare back exposed where her sweater lifts. But her hands and face tell her age—she's pointed this out herself, adding, with a tight smile, it was Kirk who originally spoke those words to her. Of course she never forgave Kirk for it—until the moment, she said, when they both understood it truly couldn't matter anymore. Clacka clacka clack. Soon he hears guitar, flamenco-ish but more modern. He knows some of the artists. Los Romeros, Bream, Paco Peña. Lately she's fixated on a certain acoustic quality, Ponce, Tárrega, Sor, Albéniz. Pensive, wistful. She finds some of them on Pandora. He complains to her that the music is sappy, and sometimes he makes fun of it—drooping his face, smacking his wrist theatrically against his forehead. She looks at him. How you can say that? she finally asks. It's the only thing that makes sense anymore, she says.

He can't admit to her that the music cuts him open, that he fears it. It's too beautiful; it's desolate. It makes him think of a deserted café in the middle of a baking day—shadowed by imposing bodies, dark, blurred, commanding.

Castillos de España. He knows what she's up to. Ambience. Dear creature. But he's lived long enough that behind the chords something faintly comic now whispers, at a pitch only older ears can hear. Succumbing to the music, tumbling down its vortex— that's for the young. They can afford to make messes: none will yet be final.

He'd never dream of telling Fran this. Not worth the debate that would follow.

She flounces back into her chair. So. Travel.

She arranges herself to sit on one folded leg, the other flung across the folded knee, hoists the beer, eyes on him as she drinks, tucking a curl behind an ear. Frannie, in a chair, is like kinetic sculpture. From the boombox, between fierce threshings of strings, the guitarist smacks the wood of the instrument, a resonant slap.

She prompts him: Your fear?

Ollie's chest constricts.

What?

She speaks carefully, as if to a child. Your—fear—of—travel. *Run, flee, invent an appointment, get in the car.*

He laces his hands on the table like someone interviewing for a job. Travel, he says, clearing his throat. Yes. Certain kinds.

The guitar thrums, rich and urgent, tossing his words into the air like tissue from the points of a bull's horns.

All at once, it's too much. The black bag of panic descends, a hood thrust over him. Lightless, airless. Stuck. *Get out, get out.*

His voice becomes small. Frannie—can we take a walk, please? Just a quick one?

She startles. Why of course, sweetie. Of course. Stands, takes a parting swallow of beer, screeching back the chair.

I'll just grab a jacket. And I've gotta pee. She paces off.

In three steps he is out the door (remembering to duck) onto the air-giving porch, reassuring movement of street traffic. Inhale. Sunday, late afternoon, soft, cool. Faint woodsmoke. He exhales deeply, rolls his shoulders, his mind banging like a flapping door.

How to convey it to her? How to talk about it? Other people speak of these matters joyfully—ruddy, bristling with certainty. With no flicker of qualm they plot trips to India, Brazil, Cambodia. They parachute into God knew where, hearts filled with eagerness, and he's never heard any declare later that they had not found everything they'd wanted. Perhaps it was only that no one dared confess disappointment. True, he'd once managed to bring himself to Mexico with Kirk. Yet that had failed to inoculate him against—

The menace. Murderousness.

Breathing in the darkness around the edges. A formless id, a hating, free-ranging will to destroy him. Only money kept it at bay. And sometimes even money failed. Because money was also the draw.

That was the secret at the heart of it. All travel. Everywhere.

They watch their feet, stepping high over the spiky eruptions in sidewalk where roots thrust, buckling and cracking the cement into thick, slanting plates. Early spring. Afternoon air like cream up here, sky a secret, shy blue as if surprised to find itself naked so soon. Feathers of cloud line its far edges. They watch the old houses floating past, each a pearlescent version of its original paint, scoured by time and weather. Cats curled on porches open an eye. Some stand immediately and pad out to greet Fran and Ollie as if it were a boring job. They wind their plush bodies between Fran's ankles, fur gleaming, tails a question mark.

Hello pretty, she croons, reaching down to stroke them, out to the tips of their tails. They arch their backs, irritable, interested. Her melody is devoted. Ooh yes you're pretty, *what* a pretty girl. Now go back home, pretty. Go on home.

Oddly, huge sections of autumn leaves around town have not yet dropped. Rain has usually scraped these away by now but that kind of storm is still due: many trees still sport full profiles in lifeless hues, like a dead person's hair. A few leaves the color of mercurochrome twinkle down slowly, confused, in late daylight. Spring has no place for them. Gingko's tiny blades, once the gold of Monopoly money, now blackish brown, resemble shed insect wings. Oak, chestnut, mulberry drop starfish-shaped calling cards. Some few, against reason, still hold their Halloween colors: wine, berry, popsicle.

Fran bends to gather one, holds it up to him, shading her eyes with the other hand. Bizarre, aren't they? I put them in my car, on the dash, living art, and in two minutes they shrivel and disintegrate.

Ollie lifts a brow.

She reads his look, and dismay clouds hers. Oh, dear. Sorry, sweetie. Everything points that way, doesn't it? Seasons themselves. A conspiracy. Yikes.

She plants her fists on her hips, narrowing her eyes at him. Well, fuck's sake—why don't we face this down a minute, Ollie? What's the use of letting it take over?

She begins walking again out ahead of him, fast, hands pushed into pockets. The street's almost deserted. A kid wearing smartphone wires and baggy shorts bikes past, standing on the pedals, humming. Someone's screen door falls shut.

Ollie pivots, and in a couple of long strides catches up with her. Her words have set up an ache in his chest. She is right, of course. All the logic is hers. And she's the widow, for heaven's sake. It should be him propping her.

What about our rules? she asks after a moment. Remember our rules?

Rules for aging, Ollie says, surprised. They'd devised the joke at dinner years ago—distant now—and it became a running gag, kept up for months whenever anything prodded them with its obviousness. Kirk had goosed it up, conniving new versions. They'd made themselves laugh very hard. Then Kirk had died, and the game, and its topic, vanished.

Right. Let's review them, Ollie-my-love. Perfect time for it, hey? No better time could there be. She eyes him sideways, elbows him gently. Her steps are short; his own, exaggerated. His torso holds still while his legs bend, each limb reaching out and gliding the stiff torso forward as if it rode legless on a gurney, like R. Crumb cartoons. Or that's what Fran has observed. Ollie's name, she's told him more than once, should have been Ichabod.

She prompts him. So how did we start?

No body odor, he says carefully. And then the coincidence of his earlier plea to her, that she alert him if he starts to smell, smacks him. He flashes her a *see-I-told-you-so* look, after which he can't help smiling at the sidewalk as he presses forward.

No dragon-breath, he adds, remembering faster. (Quickly, while she is not looking, he cups his palm to his mouth, puffs out and sniffs it. Seems okay.)

No hair poking from wrong places, she is saying.

No food stains. No bag-lady clothes. No fridge full of moldy science projects.

They round a corner. The neighborhood's dappled with new life. Quince is out, strawberry-colored petals on austere black branches. Camellias, masses of them, crayon red and pink. African tulips just opening, white cups. Brazen yellow daisies. Wisteria already tumbling in clusters of lavender bubbles down pillars and trellises. Even the rosemary bushes are covered with tiny, blueish blossoms. First irises, to his amazement, poke from troweled earth: purple velvet.

No flaking, Fran continues.

And if you start to lose your hearing, he says, immediately get a hearing aid.

Correction, Fran says. Immediately get a *God-damned* hearing aid, the best you can afford. She squints ahead of them, pleased, hands balled in jacket pockets. He's always liked that jacket, brown corduroy with a sheep's wool collar. When he admired it aloud, she thanked him: Kirk bought it for her in Idaho.

No talking to people with your eyes closed, he offers.

No speeches about malfunctioning body parts. Or diets. Or meds. She turns to grin at him.

No blow-by-blows of surgical procedures, he says, smiling back.

No displays of scars.

Or dental work!

They pass a house shaped like a long church, painted the color of a school bus. In the yard a tricycle, a deflated soccer ball, several dead plants in pots. Or maybe, he thinks, the plants are still hibernating.

Ollie's voice grows dreamy, admiring a queue of orange California poppies just unfurling: so bright they seem to own an extra dimension.

No bitterness about the passage of time, he says.

They're heading northeast, toward the historical district—Victorian mansions sitting widely spaced and immaculate, like fancy cakes. Those yards will be parklike, straight from magazines. She knows he loves looking at them.

No refusing to deal with new technologies, she says.

No whining about how much better things were in the past.

Or weathermen being wrong, she says.

Or about traffic.

Or infrastructure.

Or taxes.

Or fashions.

Or the cost of stamps. Or how late the mail comes.

No carping at the young for being young, he adds—his face heating. *Guilty, terribly guilty.*

Her gaze still happily distant, she adds: No hating them for having fun.

They look at each other then, and blurt in unison: *You kids get off my lawn!*

She stops at the edge of the walk, the busy intersection they will cross, and has to prop her hands on her knees she is laughing so hard, her great, rude, throaty laugh. He stops to hold his ribs, helpless with laughing: looking at her only stokes it, knowing what's occurring to her—the smacking noises of piggish disapproval they always make to punctuate the lawn remark, angry gumming sylla-bles suggesting the utterer is deaf—*eh? heh?*—and more toothless, smacking noises. He feels his eyes crinkling shut and his face break open in tearful, diaphram-squeezing gasps, and for a breathless instant all his own fusty trembling sadness, the full whinging, hand-wringing lifetime of it, crumbles away. Cars blur past in both direc-tions, an ugly soundtrack of engines, and he and Fran are doubled over; people's faces behind car windows mildly mark the two of them. How he loves what happens when they laugh like this! The swooning weakness, the helpless giving in, the swept-clean, cham-pagne air that fills him afterward. Why can't this feeling live in him longer? Why can't it just stay put after it erupts, carpet his insides like clover—or like some timed-release drug? Well, of course it is a drug, laughter chemicals. He still channel-surfs for stand-up com-edy, hoping to pry some of those chemicals loose: the comedians always so young—who else would risk what they risk?—saying absurd, vulgar things that pinch him just so. Sometimes vulgar is better. When it succeeds he laughs exactly the way he'd craved, then goes to bed pleasantly wracked—unable, even just afterward, to remember a single word of what made him laugh.

They straighten up and wipe their eyes, cars zipping back and forth; they look at each other sighing, little disbelieving murmurs of pleasure. Fran's cheeks and nose are pink.

Oh, she says, sniffing, running the back of her hand under her nose, the heels of her palms under her eyes. Oh.

Frannie, he shouts over the clamor of rushing cars, searching all his pockets for a handkerchief. I'm a fool.

She touches his arm, making him pause to glance at her.

Horseshit, he sees her mouth say.

Kitchen lights across the black moat of yard, through the privet branches, from the open window next door. Good.

From her bedroom, through the louvers, the light is whey-colored, medical, often late into the night, sometimes all night. It soothes her. A bunch of young men rent the house, the kind she called jocks in high school. Now they themselves teach high school jocks, or tend bar, or sell smartphones or memberships in fitness centers. Three or four of them—she's never sure how many. Different cars, trucks, motorcycles. They wave, arriving and departing, mowing the lawn, dragging out trash bins. She waves. They used to wave at Kirk, who'd shout a friendly greeting, joke with them. Their television, a giant screen digital, flickers cartoon colors through the home's front window every night, scraps of this also visible through her bedroom blinds. It pleases her to think of the young men coming and going, eating and drinking, raking leaves, screaming at sports on television, having sex with visiting girlfriends (inaudibly, thank God). Sometimes in the early morning, opening the blinds in her own front room, she spots a young woman in tight jeans, mussed and smeared, her off-the-shoulder top hanging wrongly, wobble from their front door in stiletto heels, slip into her car, creep it away. This makes Fran feel very old.

The boys give backyard parties—music that vibrates her teeth; young men *haw*ing, girls squealing and cackling half the night. The young men's shouts have a maddened, hoarse, animal quality, as if they might any second start tearing one another to pieces. Their sound saddens her; tells her the world has begun its grinding work on them—also, inseparably, that the only thing the boys can conceive of wanting, the only thing that can possibly calm them over these bereft hours, is to screw themselves senseless. Each of those goliaths, she tells herself, was once someone's plump, baby-powder-smelling darling; joy-drenched, gummy grinner. But their shouts unnerve her. It's not so much the language—she is herself the queen of foulmouthing. It's the rage. When she'd complained to Kirk he always reminded her it could be much worse; these parties happened seldom and usually on Saturday nights—standard night for letting be, for loosening up. *Good lads,* he'd concluded. Kirk was right. It's true they're mostly quiet. They have jobs. They keep up the yard. They hire a house-cleaning service: she's seen the car pull up during the day, unload two or three chattering, messy-haired women toting buckets and bottles. Flags appear on patriotic holidays; white lights drape the facade during Christmas break. Good lads. Fundamental, even decorous, mostly, the life of the place next door. The constancy of it consoles her. If something happened—though the worst has already happened, and God knows there's no point inventing scenarios—they'd race to help.

She peers through the louvers another moment, trying to identify certain objects in the kitchen through the dividing hedge. A green glass bottle—its shape first suggested cheap wine but lately she's revised that guess: probably vinegar, since it's always there. And some brown bottles, one the unmistakable shape of Grand Marnier. It would make sense. A plastic bag of sandwich bread. Sometimes she sees only fragments of people gathered in the kitchen, the interfering louvers making the visible parts float like separate pieces: an elbow here, a shoulder there, a Picasso painting. Now and again a large, headless being—the top of their window cuts it off—stands at the window facing her, arms moving busily left-center-right, scrubbing motions. So the sink's there, below the window. Sometimes, during these dishwashing scenes, she can see the tender hollow at the base of a young man's neck. This makes her feel hapless, akimbo. She tightens her louvers so they can't see her undressing for bed—Christ knows they'd regard the idea with horror—and digs behind the pillow for her pajamas.

•

At the beginning, bed was the default. The only truth. She'd lain on the bed, dressed or not, hours, days. Light followed dark. Listening to nothing, seeing nothing, no thoughts or will. Only a wordless replay, again and again behind her forehead—like one of those art show installations, repeating film loops—of the slumped figure of her husband on the living room couch. He had been helping her fold laundry while watching football, his half-folded sweatpants spilled from his hands, pants he always wore to the gym, one leg of them opened across the floor, the game still roaring in the background like a packed coliseum—she'd never remembered to turn it off—followed by the ambulance, the hospital, the milling faces she'd never identified, noises and machinery and movement, murmuring. Followed by silence.

She steps into the green bottoms and pulls them up, not bothering to tie the tie.

Mail collected, stained and wrinkled from weather. The neighbors from the other side finally stacked and ordered it, placed it in a sealed plastic bag and left the bag, alongside covered containers of food, at the foot of the front door. They also began mowing her lawn, front and back.

Phone messages piled up. Voices.

She'd lain in bed, eyes open. There'd been a stunning mistake. Galaxy-sized, cosmic. Some wrongful confusion, identities mixed up. Everything at home was just as it had been; his shirts and jeans in the closet, his checkbook on his desk (his lists, which she has kept: *through 6/22, 180 lbs., carwash, finish Fukuyama book, lawn*), the half-and-half for his coffee in the fridge. Kirk was about to step back in from the gym or the grocery store, h'lo-h'lo!, or from a Boys' Night with his pals where he'd stayed over to sleep it off, making sure he tucked in the scrambled eggs and sausage and coffee before he left. But not only did no one seem to understand this gigantic, crazy-ass error—everyone seemed to be colluding with it, eyes and voices lowered, squeezing a forearm or shoulder, looking elsewhere, backing away. And slowly she sank into the slow-motion, silent film of what had once been an effortless unreeling, all noise and color. Objects stood still.

Absence of movement, absence of sound. A stopping. Silence in her teeth, in her bones. Nowhere to appeal for a retrial—this impossible, tawdry version of someone else's script.

She reaches into each sleeve of the flannel top. Ollie came at once after Kirk died. She had no living relatives—the family stump, she called it. There was no one she felt close to in town, even after nearly twenty years here with Kirk. Her two best friends in the city, from her life before him, had since moved out of state. Each had offered by phone to fly in but she told them no: she'd seen neither in so long, the prospect, in her catatonic state, of making up for lapsed years while explaining the unthinkable present overwhelmed her. Ollie showed up within an hour of her call. He stayed a week on the futon in the front room, flung his long sleeping bag there: navy blue, a blue-and-green hunting-shirt plaid for its soft lining. He made her eat: soup and toast and salad, boiled eggs. Made her coffee, gave her the sedative at night (placing the pill container in a high cupboard in the kitchen afterward), led her to the bathroom each morning and shut her in with orders that she bathe. While she did, bewildered, stupid, he pulled clean clothes from her closet and drawers, and laid them on her bed. He walked her around the block slowly that first week, holding her upper arm with both his hands as they took steps. She'd moved like an old woman. They sat together in the backyard if it was warm enough, listening to birds, drinking tea. Ollie had resembled a mournful sentry in a Shakespeare play: head bowed, eyes inward, mouth set in a line. She cannot imagine what she looked like. She couldn't see correctly for a while, it seems, because she has no recollection at all from that time of her own image in mirrors. Maybe she avoided mirrors. After those first days he came once a week for a while, bringing dinner. Then once a month. Then he phoned once a month, his voice patient and careful.

Ollie resumed his Ichabod life. And as is true of all who've dwelt in shock and lived on, she began to absorb, like a slow-drip chemical, the cosmic mistake. Consciousness returned, limpingly; days accrued at no speed, without distinction, like wet sand drizzled onto itself. Ollie drove her to the bank and the market because at first she could not drive—she had the conviction the car would float away as if in river rapids, no matter how she turned the steering wheel or pushed at the brake. Kirk's union rep came to the house and gave her a package of papers; he explained matters very gently. A one-time death benefit, a monthly pension. Kirk had made sure she would have the house, enough to live on. She listened to the rep, thanked him. The house so still around them as he spoke, it seemed to be listening, too. She listened to the listening house. Her responses felt, much of the time, as if she'd just stood up after sitting for months in a darkened theater: dizziness, torso and legs stiff, eyesight pixillated with a hundred tiny light-flashes.

When she met people, she made polite sounds. Fine, thank you. Thank you for asking, fine. *Please,* she would mentally implore them, *please go away now.*

The odd thing was, she remembered *being* them. Meeting individuals who'd lost someone. Trying to say something helpful, to stand, for a minute anyway, inside their loss with them— but she remembers that even while she made sorrowing sounds at them her mind would already have flown, impatient, careening, scanning the far countryside of her own obsessions, annoyed by the temporary roadblock of the unfixable thing, casting about for something to say, knowing no words she could scrape from her mind's buzzing walls would sound right or even sincere, let alone stick. Her falseness was despicable. She'd marveled at it even back then, before the tables turned. But even the marveling itself couldn't last long, because dailiness swept her on, swept everyone on. She could no more resist it, the dailiness, than hold steady in a riptide.

Then dailiness became her jailer.

It took a year before she stopped smelling him the instant she opened the door to enter the house. Hair-oil smells, frying smells, paper page smells, rubber and sweat from his sneakers, from his workout clothes stuffed in the sports bag. She buried her face in these. The faint, agreeably oniony smell of his body.

Busy, alive smells. They would hit her full force as she stepped in, brought her nearly to her knees.

A lot of time spent wandering in and out of rooms, staring at things. Photos, paintings. Pens and dulled pencils bunched in an old ceramic mug. Every object, of course, had its story: the monograph, the Italian spoon-rest, the gourd painted in delicate wine-and-evergreen iridescence. A small African carving, dark gray stone. Books stacked in neat piles on the side table by his leather chair, reading he'd meant to get to. Biographies. Peter the Great, Cicero. She would lift a cover, see his name scribbled on the flyleaf, drop the cover. Everything sat exactly where it had always sat: his *Saveur* and *Economist* overlapped, orderly and straight, on the coffee table. She could not think of moving the magazines, the books. She knelt before his chair, lay her head against the seat cushion.

In the kitchen she would take a few steps, stop, stand very still. Pull out a drawer, stare at the cutlery: his best knife, still stowed in its protective casing. The knife used to terrify her. She never failed to point out, when he crushed garlic cloves under the laid-flat blade with his palm, that she had absolutely no desire to drive him to the emergency room. A deeper drawer held the big tools. Ladles, spatulas, tongs, prongs, baster, mixer—hopeless tangle of silver and plastic, like a cache of weapons from an early civilization.

She opened pantry cupboards. Kirk had loved to put by, top them up, forever shopping for bulk at discount, making them feel fortified, sandbagged against want. Sardines, herring—the reeking sandwiches he loved—smoked oysters. Bags of pasta, canned tomato sauce. A king-sized carton of instant oatmeal in three flavors. Dried beans: pinto, black, and white. Two kinds of rice, enormous sacks. He'd been trying so valiantly to move away from meat. Jars of curry sauce, chutney, boxes of tea. Olive oil, extra virgin. Peanut sauce, teriyaki sauce, barbecue sauce in giant plastic jugs. The freezer packed with bagged cuts of meat, chicken, fish. Stews, meal-sized portions. Sausage like frozen penises. She touched none of it. Ancient bits of onion skin still littered the cupboard floor where he'd kept a wire basket of them; the few onions left had rotted peaceably there until she'd discovered them one day, the sight an accusation so violent (spheres of black ash which collapsed at a touch) it had made her heart seize. Trembling, she'd slid a newspaper under the basket and dropped the whole package into the outside trash.

Dragging the trash bins out, she felt most keenly wronged. Dusty and they stank, cobwebs attached, spiders busy. He'd always dragged the bins out, and back in. He'd always fixed the stuck drains, sawed off dead tree limbs, driven stakes into the ground and tied the young oleander straight so it wouldn't stick out too far into the driveway. And the garden—but she could not go near it yet. Later. Later.

For a long stretch she lived in silence. The drone of an overhead plane, the neighboring dog's yips, water from the tap, her loafer soles on linoleum. Music, in any form, struck her as a kind of atrocity. No radio. She tried television late at night but found it baffling, every channel like a bad acid trip, a different cage at the zoo. Only after many months, in the course of her aimless walks through the rooms of the house, did she stop one morning at the shoeboxes of CDs and begin flipping through them, studying covers and titles like faces of almost-forgotten friends. Most of these recordings she had once been able to play note for note inside her head, often just at the sight of the CD's cover. She chose Satie first. Listening was like watching a twist of incense smoke. It fitted her cold, inverted sense of things, the cramping stomach, the bleak harlequin slant. After more time she could play the others, beloved to her in the past—but now she heard them differently, as if the sounds came from a distant room. After still more time she could remember exactly what she had loved about certain music, how time and motion stopped when the sounds soaked into her. Now a curious tenderness arose for this earlier self, this ardent being.

She watches herself in the long mirror, buttoning the pajama top. Glad to see collarbones, a visible clavicle. She is still slim and strong, but if you looked closer—she catches herself quickly: it matters nothing.

Now it's she who phones Ollie, poking at him, annoying him.

At the beginning, she couldn't decide how to feel about him. Kirk brought home all kinds of strays. Often he met them in bars or on airplanes. Oh, the trouble he courted! Once he told her about stepping off a plane for a conference in Singapore blind drunk, his seatmate having bought him drink after drink. Thank Christ he'd retained the wits to decline a last-minute gift of marijuana—the plastic baggie held out toward him, the idiot seatmate grinning, in the precise moment the plane taxied toward the arrival gates. Possession in Singapore was punishable by death. Yet Kirk seldom met anyone who didn't interest him. *Pub Guy* had been her nickname for him, some moments uttered fondly; others with tart irony. And when, as occasionally happened, a strange couple from Melbourne or Manchester or Lille stood on the front porch peering through the screen door, duffels in hand, her stomach would drop, and she'd curse the whole marriage enterprise. She'd felt at times as though she served in a kind of domestic army reserve, recruited without notice to be a sort of western Jackie Kennedy, to present and preside, grace and facilitate. Guests lolled on their furniture drinking their beer, absorbing favors like porous fungi. Meals, long chats, rides, tours of the region. The fight with Kirk, always the same one—*Why do I have to like these people? Where is it written; what law? Why do we entertain more than everyone we know combined?*—when he would gaze long minutes at her in amazement, as though he were only truly beginning to comprehend that he'd married a werewolf—that fight would have to wait until their guests had departed.

This Oliver character had been recruited (mutually, it seemed) as a travel partner in Mexico, long before she'd met Kirk. She'd amused herself for years, once Ollie had been introduced to her, picturing how he and Kirk must have looked wandering the desert together: Simon and Garfunkel, no doubt of it, albeit a Garfunkel with a shaved head. Yet she hadn't been able to begrudge this gaunt being, whose entire posture seemed to apologize. Ollie was so tall he had to duck through the front door, making her feel like some underground hobbit welcoming him to her burrow. Often he sat on the floor when the three of them lounged in the living room. She'd urge him to take a seat on the couch or put a big pillow under his non-ass, but he wouldn't budge from the bare wood floor—perhaps because it minimized his height, his long back curved against the wall, wineglass carefully placed where he hoped no one would kick it, his face turning from her to Kirk as each of them spoke, listening with fierce attention, speaking little himself. That's still her strongest memory of Ollie: him sitting on their floor, his face working as if to decipher a slightly foreign language. It makes her fondness surge, but also, even now, pricks her—that troubling prick of annoyance. She could not imagine how sitting that way did not hurt, why he'd *elect* that. His head oddly eggish, shaved. Startled-looking, when he wasn't in a despondent fog. And his habit of saying *What?* in a manner so pained, so abrupt—popeyed with alarm—struck her as borderline rude, though of course Ollie would never mean to act rudely. Either his reveries went so deep he didn't hear things the first time, or possibly he needed a hearing aid—despite their rules for aging. Maybe it was an unconscious way of distancing. She couldn't make herself bring it up, even after all this time.

She pulls on the favorite socks (hot pink, spongy). The dance of bedtime prep. Is it possible to love domestic rituals too much? The pajamas, robe, the ablutions. The favorite mug (white china shaped like a cardboard franchise cup, fitted rubbery cap to hold in heat). Padding from room to room. The vitamins, the tea. Habits of cleaning, opening mail, shaking hot sauce onto food. Was it possible to lose one's whole self, past and future, all one's critical faculties, inside these comforting movements? Especially when no husband stood guard to check her: *What are you doing? Why are you bothering with that? It doesn't need that. I wouldn't bother with that. Have you absolutely got everything you need before I lock this door?*

Yes. Everyone warned about it. Even Kirk had warned about it: sinking into the suckhole of ease. If so—if small motions and objects, cozied in ritual, destroy whatever may be left of an edge— then whatever edge she once possessed is long, long gone.

But the opposite trap must be equally dangerous: giving up. Letting all the balls drop. She'd felt the undertow plenty of times, the siren-strong. Pushed away from it thickly, heavily, the way you kick yourself toward the surface from a too-deep dive.

One found the worst examples—of giving up, that is—in the paper. Characters who stopped washing, stopped eating. Suffocated at home under accumulated junk, sat on park benches in their own urine.

Coziness can still morph, though, without warning. Turn inside out. Shove you into freefall. On a bad day, objects, walls, floors can choose to betray you. She can stare at a vase or a roll of paper towels and not remember, for a time, what it is. The familiar becomes suddenly leached, unknown, sickening.

Ollie surely endures more of this than she credits him for. Daily, no doubt. He never speaks of it.

She wraps up in her heavy terry robe, ties its sash.

Memo to Kirk: *Ollie is my brother now. No way around it. A dear, good, mad, exasperating, fucked-up, insoluble brother. All we've endured, separately and together, forms a weird, default country—we two alone trade its language, its currencies.*

A lonely citizenry.

She moves to the bathroom, flicks on the strong bulbs above the mirror.

One bulb is out. Gah. Difficult to find their replacements in the military vastness of Home Depot—another of the billion chores Kirk took care of.

Begins brushing her teeth, eyeing herself. As always, her gaze veers to the vertical lines etched between nostrils and upper lip. In a magnifying mirror they're a series of scaly pink canyons raking a desolate, flesh-colored planet. Yes, a lifetime of western sun. Yes, she might have tiptoed through her days covered like a beekeeper, and kept better skin. Except no, she could never have lived like that: sunbathed for years, immortal, firm and brown, slathered with baby oil. Clearly—for shame how clearly—she remembers her young smooth cocoa-colored self disdaining those accordioned upper lips on older women's faces. Disdaining them! Believing the lines proved some personal loss of control, failure of character. Failure itself. What on *earth* possessed us to think so cruelly, prosecute so illogically? Kirk, bless him, never mentioned her lines. Of course she can't forget the remark about her face and hands, but that was early on. In their last years he tried to reassure her—when they watched a movie featuring a beautiful woman he'd murmur *you're still beautiful, sweetheart.* Yet she still feels the twitchy reflex to accuse herself—those vertical lines, the net of other lines now draping her face.

She opens her jar of moisturizer, whose name promises rejuvenation. She can never decide whether the cream actually helps, or only staves off worse damage—afraid to stop using it despite its absurd price; afraid that if she stops her face will become a monster's, like Dorian Gray. As she smooths on the stuff she can never not think of an article she once read—how the late Helena Rubenstein begged women to apply face cream in upward motions: *up, up, always up.* As if that were the single, golden key. She watches the ballet of her hands, oval circles over throat and cheeks, around her eyes. *Up, always up.* Rubenstein was now ash and worms, or perhaps sea-water.

She thinks of the women queuing for restroom stalls at symphony concerts or the theater, when (rare now) she goes down to see a show in the city. Mannish, hawklike under powder and rouge, perfumes like insecticide, expensively dressed, heavy wool. Emerging from the stalls, heading for the sink, the women eye her a half-second: at the mirrors they eye themselves longer. She can't look away. Severe distaste and a kind of brisk fury in them, as if pushing through a series of obstructions. Her grandmother. Of course that's what she will become, assuming she lives that long.

At least Kirk did not have to see her become her grandmother. *Forever wilt thou love, and she be fair.*

Cruel nature, cruel humans. Cruel youth. Poor Ollie.

•

Cheeks bulging with mouthwash, she cracks open the bathroom window. Chilled, clean air pours through. She returns to the sink to spit blue liquid, not seeing the mirror anymore but Ollie, whose angular frame she stood on tiptoe to embrace a few hours ago (it felt like hugging a hat-rack) and kissed (stubbly cheeks scented with something citrusy) before he folded himself into his little Morris Minor under the cold stars—backed it from the driveway and putt-putted it home. The vehicle inherited from his folks, a rattling teapot he maintains despite the humbug of parking in the city. It backfires a lot. Inside it, he appears to be driving a bumper-car at the fair. People either grin or curse at him as they pass him on the freeway. She waved at the car as it blatted down the street, though it was dark, and she knew he wouldn't check for her retreating form in his rearview. Ollie never agrees to spend the night, even though she keeps the big futon ready—honestly a comfortable bed that would contain him, or most of him—and plenty of excellent coffee for the morning. Whenever she asks him why, he claims he feels best waking up in the city. He *needs urban,* he tells her, staring at her like a convict. Never mind how he praises the air and gardens up here, never mind he originally comes from Chicken Town. She knows, before asking, he'll decline to stay over. But she always asks.

She darkens the house, checks the locks and, taking a last glimpse at the wheyish light slatting through shuttered louvers, sloughs off her robe, inserts herself into bed. She gulps her vitamins, and commences rubbing lotion into her feet. Feet that have traveled and served, smooth heels, slight bunions—legacy of her late mother, whose demure feet were deformed into trowels by the wedgies of her day. Examines her faithful toes, cold this time of night, darker rose around the joints and edges. So many incarnations from the silken boxy extremities in baby photos, toes then like little grapes. And right after Africa—what, thirty-eight years ago, impossible—her friend Cynthia had told her, staring down at them, *your feet have changed.* And it was true; her body emptied by dysentery, her feet had become thin and pale. She kneads lotion into the arches, heels, callouses of the little toes. Dumb, sturdy loyalty of feet. Kirk used to massage them. That was not something you asked other people to do. So rare to be touched anymore that when the haircutter scrubs her skull, thumbs pressing her temples, she wants to cry out, relief like pain. She should get a massage, just up and bloody pay for it, though the prices grate her. The women at the gym talk of massages—housecleaners too—as if they were an entitlement. She keeps finding reasons to postpone it.

Daubs raspberry-flavored chapstick over her lips, tugs pajama sleeves to wrists, pulls bedclothes higher. Lying on her back she places her hands, palms up, under her thighs to warm them. The flesh of her thighs and buttocks feels like a softened inner tube.

The living flesh.

She knows what Ollie is trying, in his choked way, to tell her.

Again and again she scolds him—to pull him back to earth, make him grasp things, take hold. She's aware it's a female impulse: a man wouldn't talk that way to him, so at some level her habit must revolt him. Though Ollie doesn't hate women, exactly. More like they're a problematic species he tries to appease. It hurts her a little to see him wince when she scolds him; he's either resolving never to be frank with her again or else storing away some private, complicated punishment for himself. Maybe both. But she's convinced he needs a firm surface to butt up against, a door to slam. She owes him that. Too much cobwebbiness there, too much driftiness, the way he lets small nonsense conflate into one of his ornate nightmares. She barks to keep them both alert, defined, keep them from crumbling, floating off. Sometimes just the prospect of hauling him back, the way you'd pull someone over the side of a boat, exhausts her. Because of course she feels what he feels. She's only four years younger than Ollie. People their age natter along not copping to it but the awareness is billboarded all over their faces—a wavering, a hesitation, even those who used to crow and jab the air and own the place. The tablecloth of certainty, with all its sparkly settings, has been yanked, and not artfully. It's why people drink.

When she meets someone who still owns any wits at all, man or woman, she longs to stop all tabletalk and grab that being by the shoulders: *So how are you managing it?* Maybe the truth will pop from somebody's mouth before anyone knows what's happened.

A kind of exorcism.

She hasn't tried it yet. She imagines she's waiting for the right person, the right moment—but that's probably magical thinking.

She sighs, turning on her side, drawing up her knees. The sheets feel icy.

She used to buttonhole Kirk about this stuff. Of course they were younger then. He'd burst out laughing at the difference between them. His thoughts would have been traipsing the gentle hills of whether to make fettucine or risotto, what game was on next, how close it was to four o'clock so he could have the day's first beer. She understood, of course, the comic target she made. *Eeyore,* he teased her. *Ibsen's poster-girl.* Diving to the bottom of the pond and holding on. Listening to her, he'd struggle to keep his laughing mouth straight—often while sautéing onions and garlic, filling the kitchen with mouthwatering steam, checking his oven, breaking eggs, heaping flour, measuring, whisking, chopping, glass of wine to hand. Stacking the tower of crusted, greasy pans and bowls she'd later attack piece by piece, a mess that would require rubber gloves and three kinds of cleaning solvents and SOS pads.

If she kept at her worrying, Kirk would lift his brows and catch her eye and cock his face, pointing a ladle at her. *Same pants,* he'd remind her in a warning tone. It was shorthand: *You've got the same pants to get happy in.* An adage handed him, whenever he whined or complained, by his late ma, a tough little toiler who'd scraped and scrabbled, like everyone else on that bombed-to-shit island after the war, for enough to eat, an occasional cigarette. A life so bone-bare that war rationing *improved* her family's diet. The entrenched slogan those years—still the admired stand—had always been *get through it.* Which translated handily, if you thought about it, to the American *get over it.*

It used to infuriate him, Kirk had said, when his ma threw the *same pants* pronouncement at him. She'd be drying dishes, her face assuming an airy superiority, like a lawyer with an air-tight case. What set his ears flaming as a kid (and what he couldn't admit) was that for a good while, he wasn't entirely sure he understood. Gradually, he said, it seeped in. If the rest of existence does not really care a fuck, and all other givens stay the same—why not please yourself?

Long as you're doing nothing criminal, he'd add. Or too kinky.

(Here Kirk's brows always danced a Groucho-waggle, lecherous, disgusting; he'd start pawing at her, all grabby fingers. Same pants, *no pants,* he'd growl. No! Fran would yell, laughing and twisting away, pushing him off. Get away from me!)

The phrase drew the line under all other sums. The *touché* that couldn't be bested.

Also, Kirk knew, it never failed to make Fran laugh.

She curls up tighter in the silence. Too cold to get comfortable. Fuck.

With a little snort of effort she rolls sideways, leaves the bed, fetches the heavy robe, spreads it over the top of the bedclothes like a settled parachute, reenters the bedclothes. She'll be too hot in a moment, and throw it all off.

llie has just turned off his hot-dust-smelling reading light, adjusted his mask, punched his earplugs in deeper and positioned the rolled pillow between his legs while assuming the fetal curl in the dark, when the bedside phone rings.

The sound—a shrill, witless bleat—frightens him so much (even through earplugs) that his torso and shoulders jump: both his arms prickling with adrenalin. He can never bring himself to turn off the phone, even for sleep. What he imagines he'll miss by turning it off, he can't say. He dreads calls. Telemarketers, electioneers, firemen and cops shilling for donations. Worst are acquaintances trying to show an interest—birthdays, lunches, tea—crossing it off their to-do lists once they've dialed his number. Or the few old Castro friends (embarrassing how some had let themselves go; fat draped like excess dough over the waistbands of their assless chaps)—wanting to check out the billionth re-release of *Fantasia* or *Gone with the Wind* or the original *Mildred Pierce*. Sometimes it's former students or people he knew from school. He doesn't wish them ill, but he can't think of anything to say to them beyond the usual niceties. He relies on the machine to collect calls, like a roach trap—and on the fact that the caller is often identified on the handset. He never phones anyone back. He hopes people will assume, when they do not hear from him, that he is traveling, or too senile to remember to follow up—the rare instance, he thinks sourly, when age might work in one's favor.

Another electrified bleat. He pries the sticky plugs from his ears, flicks the light, pulls himself across the bed toward the handset in its sleek, space-age base, a comic-strip apparatus from a future he now inhabits. Seizing his spectacles, he holds them like lorgnettes to make out the name on the screen in spider-thin print.

Fran Ferguson.

For Lord's sake. This late? He snatches up the handset and presses the green button with his thumb, struggling with his other hand to loop the spectacle earpieces behind his ears.

His heart's still a tom-tom.

Fran—his voice breathless, heart punching—for heaven's sake what is it? Is everything all right?

Perfectly groovy, thank you. Just pipping. Ollie?—she breezes ahead with no pause—did you know that Jane Fonda, who is about 80 years old now, stands five feet eight and weighs one hundred twenty-one pounds? And looks like a billion dollars?

He takes the first stabilizing breath. Clamping the receiver against his ear, he uses his free hand to shove three pillows into a pyramid, wriggling up against the pile so it will support his back. He removes the specs, closes his eyes, exhales.

No, Fran. I didn't know that.

It seems to me, Fran says—heedless of his rejoinder—that money has everything, everything to do with this. Knee replacement, hip replacement, facial work. Fonda admits to it. Magazine article. Found it at the gym. Blanking on the name—

Let her have her bit of theater, he tells himself. Give her her timing. It's making one of us happy at least. And neither of us has to wake early. (Except he likes to be up by eight to feel he is not letting the day get past him, and he likes to have at least nine hours of sleep, which has already, with this call, been curtailed.)

He keeps his voice even.

Yes, Fran. The money. That does, indeed, sound likely.

So if money can accomplish the crudely physical, Fran says— her language sounds rehearsed to him, words she's been telling herself—then money can surely as hell, at the same time, give a jump-start to the metaphysical. Don't you think?

What?

She's lost him. Thank God he doesn't own a cell phone (though she hounds him all the time about getting one) or he'd be dealing with this everywhere he went. She carries hers in her bra, which makes him laugh: when it rings, her breast sends out the stagey *bing-bong* of a high-end doorbell.

Um, Fran, I'm sorry but—may I wonder—

Tell me something, Ollie. When was the last time *you* heard anyone going around whistling or singing, for no obvious reason?

And something else. When was the last time you whistled or sang for no obvious reason?

Her words like a smart slap, followed by the creeping heat of his blush. Ridiculous, but he feels denuded. Stripped.

A long pause. His bedroom so still. Occasional shirring in the street as a car passes. A siren across town. In his ear, the whoosh of Fran's exhales through her nostrils. It must be even quieter in her bedroom. He's tried to discourage himself from speculating too much about Fran's preoccupations these latter years, because nothing in his own past compares fairly with hers. She had sixteen years of domestic life with a spouse. He had a couple of years of furtive visitations, at best, with Ennis. A fruitless line of thinking.

After a pause, presumably to allow him time to speak and then satisfy herself that he will not, she continues.

Me neither, Ollie. I can't remember hearing anybody singing or whistling since forever. At least not in my neighborhood. It happens so seldom it just about clubs me over the head when it does. And Christ knows I don't go around singing or whistling. So it's not like I'm trying to lord it over anybody here. I hope you can appreciate that.

He opens his mouth, thinks better of it, closes it. Glances at the little clock. Near midnight.

It seems to me, Fran is saying, that I remember that people went around singing aloud—

Yes, Fran, he says quietly, closing his eyes again. In Bologna.

Bologna? She sounds confused, thrown off her script. He can hear sticky shifting noises; probably passing her phone into the other hand.

After Kirk's Florence semester, Ollie says. Right after he was done teaching and you'd begun traveling. You and Kirk were walking past shops, arcades. Beautiful old buildings, you said, but graffiti everywhere. A sunny Sunday morning; the university was letting out for the year. And a bunch of boys were cruising down the middle of the street, singing the song "Hey Baby." *I wanna know . . . if you'll be my girl.* The boys sang it together on key, in perfect English. Then you both boarded a bus, I think, and as it pulled into the street the boys walked behind the bus, waving and singing. You said it made you insanely happy. You said that it also kind of shamed you, because the kids had so much joy they could afford to give some away.

Quiet from the receiver.

Wow, Ollie. You remembered. I didn't think—

I know. But I do listen, Fran.

Another silent moment.

He glances again at the clock, sighing: Frannie dear, it's getting late, and I really—

She was speaking before he could finish.

What do you think, Ollie, about the idea of going there. Or somewhere like there.

In the silence that follows, she adds:

What I'm thinking—what I mean is—what about going together, Ollie.

2

Ollie wakes in half-light, to steady ticking. Surges of ticking. Pebbles hitting the window by handfuls, in bursts. It takes several beats before he understands that he is hearing rain. And that he's in Toulouse.

He pushes his mask up, blinks at the dim room. In the single bed a few feet away, parallel to his, the slight lump under bedclothes, sheets and blankets yanked completely over the form, very still. He watches it steadily for some moments to confirm the subtle fall and rise of breathing.

They'd got here, somehow, in the hardest rain he'd ever known.

It had rained in cold sheets. They couldn't see out the rental car windshield. Water hit the skin like arrows, sky blackened. They were also wearing the wrong clothes, freezing, though it was August. Fran was driving, craning forward as if that would help: swearing so furiously that had he not been frightened for their safety he would have been laughing. She pulled into one of those

Relais Routier stops, where they stood shivering in the parking lot before the yawping trunk, wrestling warmer clothes and socks and shoes from their bags as cold water pummeled them, and all around them numbers of other pained and angry citizens (*putain* and *merde* and *merdique* and more *putain*) stood before their open trunks wrestling out warmer clothes, while the stuff in everyone's open trunks got soaked.

They changed in the Routier's bathrooms. He admired the French in a thousand ways, and here was another: gas pumps out front, indoors a modest cafeteria—everything tasting wonderful—a general store stocked with sweatshirts and magazines and candy, cavernous restrooms offering dozens of stalls, even showers. He stared at the turnstiles of popular novels—he reads French so slowly—promising himself he'd buy one when he found something suitably simple. He stepped around, admiring things; bought a bag of almonds and some aspirin. They sat at a side table by the floor-to-ceiling window with their coffees and sandwiches, hugging themselves, watching the Moby Dick weather. Fran scooted her hands under her legs, hunching her shoulders.

Filthy, is what Kirk called this weather, she said. It's why he left Britain.

It would be pleasant, Ollie admitted, if we could just get warm for a while.

France had been his idea.

It's *August* for Christ's sake, she said, staring out. Maybe we should've thought more about longitude and latitude. Maybe we should've chosen Arizona.

Water streamed down the windowglass in wide rivulets. Beyond it, life moved with the tight fatalism of the trapped.

Ollie smiled weakly. Frannie, remember my Scottsdale adventure. A bunch of wealthy WASPS wouldn't have made you happy.

No, but the temperatures might have. Or Hawaii. Or the Virgin fucking Islands.

He tried again. My dear, remember we talked about wanting more difficulty than that? To deliberately try ourselves against difficulty? And how I could help with language?

She said nothing, her eyes smoky out the window.

He watched the streaming water while he chewed.

At length she drained her cup, shook her face like a dog. Okay then. Ready to run for it?

They dashed to the car, yelling, then plowed it through arcs of splashed rainwater to this city and this hotel, secured by Fran (like everything else) on the Internet: a clean, spacious monolith; two shining elevators big enough to hold a half dozen people—coffee machines in the lobby if you missed the breakfast service, which they do on purpose in an effort to avoid expense, which is of course impossible. There's a Chinese buffet around the corner and a steakhouse across the street where the sauce is so good locals start lining up outside its doors at 6 p.m. He and Frannie have walked the Canal du Midi, through parks, around the squares fronting City Hall, fountains, gardens. Toulouse feels enormous on foot, graceful with old trees, streets sinuous with moving people. Almost no Americans. Outdoor restaurants alive in early evening, air basted with aromas of roasting meat and garlic and butter, lights strung between trees, every table filled, clinking, exuberant, laughing. People adore their *vacances*.

Ollie and Fran have eaten cassoulet in trendy *caves* where it seems to be nighttime all day. They have drunk rosé and canned beer, receiving no more buzz from these apéros than from Kool-Aid. They have tossed coins into the violin cases of young men and women sawing at Bach Partitas or one of Vivaldi's Four Seasons. They have stepped carefully around the dreadlocked, cursing madmen, the schoolkids surging past in linked lines holding hands, laughing and gabbling. They have walked until they felt shin splints.

They have done these things in Bergerac, St. Étienne, and Clermont-Ferrand.

Ollie settles back, arms behind his head. His accent brings compliments. Each time a storekeeper looks sharply at him— *mais vous parlez très bien, monsieur;* Fran shoots him a *See?* look—and for a moment it fills him with shock and pleasure, echoing the day his college teacher spoke the same words. But the next moment he's on guard again, convinced he's being patronized, that he'll soon be asked something he can't understand or respond to smartly. The French speak unbelievably fast; they slur and mumble and use slang and strange regional accents. As he listens he reads an unspooling, invisible ticker tape, far slower than the way English simply opens like a flower in his comprehension. By the end of a day of reckoning with clerks and *functionnaires* and waiters his head feels wrung, but also, in a stupefied way, thrilled. Frannie stands by beaming during each transaction as if she were his agent.

He closes his eyes. He has felt men's glances. It happens with such speed no one else notices. (Fran does, *parfois*. He can feel her face checking his face. He keeps his features locked and does not turn to meet her gaze: at length she looks away, saying nothing.) The glancers aren't all chihuahuas, either, at least so far as he can make out—everyone layered up against the chill. The men are smallish but proportioned. (No one is tall here, except him.) They turn up their shirt collars, he notices, as a kind of stylish fillip, an *I'm out on the town* declaration. The men's eyes go from him to Frannie beside him (squinting up at gargoyles, balustrades, *pigeonniers*) and back to him. A wry census. *I see your game,* say their faces. *Too bad for you.* Sometimes the men ignore the prattling female at his side: their eyes send questions. He looks elsewhere, hurries on. Frannie has begged him to walk around more by himself. Insists she will not worry or scold or question if he's delayed by some mysterious—outing. He fears this, naturally, for dozens of reasons. What if his language skills lapse? What of health concerns? And where would he and any new—*liaise*—be able, exactly, to go? And then what? What object could he expect save the old standby, the dreary flash-fusion that left one adrift in a lonely haze?

He opens his eyes. The ceiling painted white, clean, efficient. For the millionth time, he misses Ennis. The cabin in the yellow hills, warm hills, long dried grass like hay, trampled where they hiked, property owned by the older man who lived in Palm Springs. (Ennis swore he and the owner had never been lovers.) In summers Ennis watched over that property—against what sort of invader Ollie couldn't imagine; mountain lions, coyotes?—in exchange for free rent. Winters there could stretch long—too cold and rainy for the uninsulated cabin. Then Ennis liked to house-sit in town, for wealthy gays who kept second homes in Forestville. A precarious life, to Ollie's thinking, and he'd worried about it, but Ennis claimed to love it. There was no reason, during that brief, blessed reprieve, to disbelieve the boy. He'd laugh at Ollie's pained face, black eyes snapping under caterpillar brows. He'd reach out and tug one of Ollie's long Babar earlobes (Ollie's heart would somersault): There's noothin I need, he'd say in soft brogue. None o' the bills, none o' the headaches. Think of payin' for storage—stuff you never use. Load of bollocks, that!

They'd met during Ollie's next-to-last year of teaching. Ennis was the gardener for the preschool. He drove a rust-laced Toyota pickup whose original color may have been yellow; now it was more like bone, all his tools and gear and an extra container of gas stacked in the truckbed. Every day when Ollie left the place they'd spot each other, Ennis bent over the shrubbery with clippers and spade. They'd nod. After a time Ollie dared to wonder whether the young man deliberately arranged his schedule to position himself there at four, when Ollie had finally finished cleaning and setting up for the next day and could leave: Ennis in gray hooded sweatshirt and jeans, crouched over a sprinkler line, snipping at hedges, shoveling to replant a cramped root system. Ollie had been so cowed by the young man's beauty he was paralyzed to speak. It was Ennis who'd at last opened the conversation, and he'd done it with teasing. The kiddies must need a ladder to say good mornin to yer, he'd offered, grinning in a pleased way. Not a speck of complexity or malice. His delight mashed Ollie's heart.

Ennis was 33 then. Ollie was 58.

Why had Ennis loved him? (Though they had never used that word.) He still couldn't say. It would take a psychologist to separate out the elements, and Ollie, during their twenty-three months together, had no wish to dissect those elements: it might disturb their effect. Ennis wouldn't describe much of his background—shied away from that, a habit of dissolving out from under Ollie's questions and remanifesting elsewhere in the room, seizing any bright diversion to change the subject. He'd only say he'd come from County Kerry and left his family, fled to the West Coast, after they'd emigrated to Boston. Ollie gathered the family had either disowned the son, or the son had cut them off. Ennis always seemed amused by Ollie—his classical music, his solemnity, his height, and never stopped teasing him about these things, but gently, without guile. Ollie thought about this for years afterward: the boy seemed to've been born without guile. In sex, Ennis had given—and seemed to receive—heavenly pleasure, the best Ollie had known, and that, too, seemed part of his guilelessness. Only it was so difficult to keep the boy near. Scarcely had they had a few hours than he'd spring up and start knocking around the room, collecting his clothes, his keys. He always had to be going, something wanted tending, he'd never say where or what. He would kiss Ollie goodbye on his neck: God bless, he say, and Ollie would die a little with the soft impress of the boy's mouth, the rough kindness of his voice, and die a little again for losing them.

Ollie wishes Ennis were with him this minute. In spite of everything. Warming him: the sour-sweet body, the starburst smile. He'd forgive him everything.

Wouldn't care if it snowed then. Would love it to snow. Stop time.

He sighed. No insult to Fran, of course.

In fact it had made both him and Fran laugh more than once, to consider the spectacle they knew they presented as a couple. The French, unamused, had a harried, brittle way of sizing them up. *Right, whatever,* said their faces. Nothing surprised the French but everything vexed them, as if he and Fran were bulky objects positioned to trip them.

We must, Fran remarked, look like a sort of circus act to them. Or mismatched condiment dispensers.

No, he'd answered sadly, just another pair of clueless American tourists. Smarting secretly at his own naïveté: he'd hoped to score a bit higher with *les indigènes.* The best he would get, apparently, would be storekeeps complimenting his accent. Fran had already got in trouble once, picking up an apple at a street-market display, unaware this was not done—only sellers handled the produce. The seller yelled at her, gesticulating at a coworker bagging people's purchases: *Let my assistant handle it, Madame; he's forty years old and fully capable, I assure you.*

Frannie had turned to Ollie: What'd he say?

He says don't touch the fruit, Ollie said, his cheeks warm.

And now they are three quarters through it, this—vacation, or odyssey. Whatever it is. While they planned it, Fran called it a fact-finding mission.

Dear God, the planning.

Those months already a century ago. Worlds ago. (He shoots his arms back under the thin blanket, tugs it to his chin, pulls the extra pillow onto his belly for warmth.) She e-mailed constantly, many times per day. (*I like to type,* was her defense.) They made list upon list, updated passports, went for unnecessary shots. An avalanche of back-and-forth, Fran cruising websites. Portable clotheslines, anti–jet lag pills (unsuccessful, as it turned out), socks that kept your blood circulating. He'd pulled out his old French grammar books, listened to cassette tapes of dated, inane conversation. Zut alors, Tante Gabrielle; j'ai complètement oublié! He found a neighbor who would let him park the Morris in her driveway and promised to start it up once a week. Fran kept e-mailing him gorgeous (retouched) photos of monuments, market tables piled with jewel-colored tomatoes and eggplants, smiling children, cake-frosting countryside and chateaux, videos of slacker boys sauntering around Paris singing *oooh, Champs Elysées.* The more she did this the more Ollie brooded: apart from the week after Kirk died, he and Fran had never spent extended time together.

He'd always avoided staying over with her. More than craving a familiar bed and private bathroom, he couldn't bear the duty, next day, of what Fran herself called *making nice.* He knows this signals trouble, symptomatic of what they've both always pledged, in their rules, to fight: closing off. Curling into a seamless pod.

And that, in fact, had been Fran's great argument for making this trip. *Cracking something open,* she said. *Getting knocked around.*

But Frannie didn't know him (he'd brooded). Not really. Nor, probably, did he know her, and in some buried chamber of his heart (may heaven forgive him this) he didn't care to. Had no wish, at this point, to really know anybody. He'd done enough knowing, the work of knowing. All he and Fran shared in the end was a habit. Not even that, because a habit meant something regular. They dabbled at contact over time, and called it a friendship. Easy to feel fond when exposure was limited. Alcohol jacked up fondness and ease, but you couldn't drink all day. And as Fran herself had always loved to point out, Jesus Christ would wear thin on you with no break in exposure. Now they'd signed on to be roped together like a couple of Matterhorn climbers. Day and night—dear Lord, the same *bathroom*—for three weeks. His anxiety had gained force. The closer departure neared, the more convinced he felt he was entering into a catastrophic mistake.

He'd waited till the day before they were to leave, to phone her.

He spoke in a whisper.

Frannie. I can't do this. I've got to cancel.

Her voice, after a beat, came back firm, bright. Perhaps a hair overbright.

Oliver Gaffney, do not be insane. Of course you're going to do this. We're going to do this together, and it will be fabulous. What can go wrong? We have credit cards. You love the language. Think of wine. Think of *coq au vin*. Think of the fucking *Red Balloon*. We'll have the best time.

His heart knocked. Honestly, Fran, I don't think I can go through with it. I'm—I'm not like you.

Sweetheart, I don't ask that you be like me. I've never asked that. But we agreed. Talked it out for so long, remember? To wake up from sleepwalking? Especially now? Time's a-wastin', dear. We're going to *France*, Ollie. We won't be held hostage. You won't be eating stale peanuts or limping away from broken-down buses. We'll sleep in hotel rooms, eat fabulous food. Beauty to pop your eyes out. And remember what Kirk always said, about the measure of anything?—*what else would you rather be doing?*

Plenty, as it happened. He'd rather, at that point, have been doing almost anything else on earth. But her quoting Kirk made him think again about his old friend. Kirk would have enjoyed this—been amused, even touched, by their effort. If only Kirk could be going with them. Kirk would have commandeered the project, lectured them, herded them around, noisy, bossy, funny—the authority on everything, the inexhaustible tour king. The hullaballoo Kirk would have made, like an obscuring dust-cloud, would have distracted Fran and sheltered Ollie—given him privacy, camouflage.

But this thinking only anguished him more. Fran did, finally, promise to bring lots of Valium. So the next day, a typical July morning in the city, foggy and chilled, he'd zipped shut his case and clicked the tiny padlock through the holes in the zipper-tags and mounted the steps into the airporter bus as if to his own hanging.

Tacktacktacktacktack. Pellets against glass. Their room's on the third floor. When you stand close to the window (a sealed rectangle like a prison window) it reveals a chunk of street, trees, dogs, passersby below. Also construction: drilling equipment, blue cordoning tape; rebar and dirt and debris gathered in cone-shaped piles at weirdly placed stations, like a pinball course. There didn't seem a town in France that wasn't ripping itself up this month, boring holes, razing buildings, upending walks—closing the most vital métro stations. Silenced today, mercifully: Sunday.

And raining.

From his bed at this distance, the window a mural of unin-flected gray, droplets pocking it in sudden droves. Grisaille.

He checks the covered form across from him. It breathes. Sighing again, he turns on his side, facing away from the form and the window.

It hasn't always been raining. They've managed to invent a series of routines. She reads the maps. He asks for information, buys tickets. They find coffee in the cafés in the morning. He eats a croissant or piece of quiche. She takes orange juice and yogurt. Lunch comes as a build-your-own from the *épiceries* or (Fran's favorite) the Monoprix deli sections. Dinner at the brasseries or inexpensive franchises. They spend all day walking, trying to see what the guidebooks cite, stopping for iced tea when they verge on collapse—always bottled Nestea, always peach-flavored for some reason, too sweet but there's no alternative, two lonely cubes of ice. The hotel rooms have been acceptable, often cramped. He dresses and undresses in the phonebooth-sized bathrooms; she begins shedding clothes as soon as she walks in with scarcely a thought to remind him to look elsewhere; he's learned to antici-pate this and turns away automatically. He sleeps in boxers and T-shirt, she in long shirts. It turns out she's rather a slob: that shouldn't have surprised him. But at her home it never fell to him to be picking up bras, panties, socks, books (*Flâneur* by Edmund White; he's dying to borrow it), town maps and newly-purchased trinkets (a large-numerals wristwatch, a straw hat) from chairs and floors, tossing them in a heap onto her bed. In many ways, though, Fran is marvelously thoughtful. She places scented can-dles in all the bathrooms. She offers him some of her Ambien when she hears him tossing around (the drug stops the flutter of panic still swimming through him at bedtime, but he dislikes the woozy residue next day). She bought him a Paul Auster novel (in French) in Tours, and a peacock-blue muffler in Amboise: stood on tiptoe to show him how to wrap it (the patient *vendeuse* stepping in after a moment to adjust Fran's arrangement). Fran's quick to pick up language. *Sportif!* she shouts, racing ahead to the spraying fountain, tossing him the camera to record her conquistador pose, one foot hoisted to the lip of the pool's rim. She can order food without making him wince. She's never complained, except about the rain. In fact she's been quieter than he expected. She's taken thousands of photos. When she shows him the captured shots on the miniature screen—he gropes for his specs each time—it almost hurts his stomach, like too much coffee, to see the pale ghoul of himself grimacing back. Why has he never before noticed the size of his nose? In the photos it threatens to take over his face. Has it grown larger?

His knee hurts. Not the kneecap, but the tendons around it.

Also, some rebel nerve in the cartilage of his right ear pings, at random moments, with a pain so sharp it makes him wince. Both shins ache, often in the middle of the night; he has to stand and walk around while bent over rubbing them—a kind of crabwalk—then fumbling to find an aspirin in his toilet case. There also seems to be a minor rash around his anus, like a rainbow around the moon. Probably stress. *En tout cas* he cannot bear to bring up this symptom for discussion in any *pharmacie.*

The France he is viewing does not quite resemble his faint, college-boy memory of chaotic Paris—but then he's never spent time in smaller cities and towns before. They are more wired than he'd anticipated, stippled with Internet cafés and elaborate cellphone outlets; even in the sleepiest *centre-villes* people walk around with the delicate phones, slim as a flatbread cracker, pressed to their ears—intensely absent, same as at home. He passes countless bling boutiques, each blaring apocalypse music and smelling of synthetic fabrics, each pollinated by clusters of anorexic young girls shouting and pushing each other. Though he gives most of his worry to navigating, he is haunted by individuals he sees in the street. Some sit on a dented suitcase that can't shut, or a plastic garbage bag. Others hang at corners panhandling, alongside several fly-ridden dogs or a dirty baby or child. *Messieurs-dames,* begins the dead voice, *s'il vous plaît.* Sometimes the kids themselves are the panhandlers, brown faces sunk in a dismay he supposes part theatrics, part default. Not everyone's begging. Many souls move past him, purposeful, but their faces and movements appear emptied. African women sheathed in Senegalese *tissu,* babies with eyes like polished obsidian strapped to their backs, gaggles of older children, trailing. The women's eyes seemed fixed on some infinite distance, without expression. Where their men are, whether there's any man at all, he dare not guess. Thin men of no figurable age who could be Egyptian or Algerian, bearing cases that fall open on a ready-made stand: neat rows of pockets containing knives, watches, cigarette lighters, phony gold and silver. They can disappear in an instant if *les flics* show up. Others, who may work for the government or the métro or the local Casino supermarket, trudge cantilevered forward, arms stretched out from their sides, plastic bags of groceries toted from each hand like buckets of milk.

Slowly the comprehension seeps through him: the menace he'd so feared before he came is not only absent from these settings—he himself may pose that menace, or perhaps a kind of bitter taunt, in the eyes of those he sees. He may as well wear a sandwich board: *I am healthy and full of wholesome food and reliable medicine, and will soon return to my homeland to resume partaking of these privileges under a fractious, gouty government that's sucking up all the resources on the planet.* He has already lived to an age greater than many of those he sees here have any hope of attaining. Though he's witnessed American scenes of want all his life and walked on, here he can't escape feeling responsible for it. And though part of him understands this thinking to be irrational and even dangerous—perhaps to invite, as if by pheromones, the sort of menace he originally feared—another part feels pulled toward it, mesmerized by it, and it exhausts him.

He hasn't broached the matter with Fran. When he tried—they were eating lentil salads on a concrete partition near the Cathédrale St. Étienne, under clouds piled like a Raphael painting's—her face went fatalistic. Kirk would say they're better off here than they would be in dozens of other places, she said. Ollie recognized the words. He'd heard Kirk say them in Mexico, too—but they'd never made him feel easier. It shouldn't surprise him that Fran isn't fazed, but neither is she insensible. Her face flinches each time they pass a begging mother or piss-smelling bum. Often he's watched her dash into the nearest *boulangerie,* return with a *croissant au chocolat* she then thrusts into hand of one or another grifter. Gazing only briefly at Ollie when she catches up with him, her face warning him to keep silent.

There is something else about what he's seeing. Something so strange he could never explain it, not to her or anyone, not even Ennis or Kirk were they to magically reappear—least of all Ennis or Kirk. It had been true in Mexico, too. The unnameable thing was a cousin of menace. A desolation. A sullen, dismal aura blanketing even the loveliest towns and chateaux. Even if the towns boast universities and big corporations—sometimes more so then. He could hardly explain it to himself. But it came at him in the way sunlight fell on land and buildings, in the angles of rooftops, shuttered windows at noon, huddled movements of people along walkways or across a square or in line at the market; it came in the cruel way older children laughed, the deadened faces of clerks and waiters and the elderly—even local animals, cats and dogs that slunk and skittered. It entered him like an injection; made him feel slightly ill. Maybe the entire business was his own projection, his simple inability to adjust to a foreign atmosphere.

An ugly American.

Certainly the *tallest* American in any direction.

They have one more day here. Then they'll take twelve days, as a final flourish, in Paris. Secretly, he rejoices that the journey is nearly over. But he must not let that show.

His teeth feel slimy. He must get up soon to scrub them—risk waking Fran—in order to grab the bathroom first. The area near his lower incisor has been bleeding when he flosses. It frightens him, the sudden freshet of bright red over his gums.

*T*ry ourselves against difficulty. Ah.

The shallow-breathing form beneath the bedclothes keeps very still, but does not sleep.

Whose imbecile idea was that? Whose merit-badge nonsense was that?

Damnation if it wasn't yours, Kirkie my love. At least originally. And your dutiful wife, loving handmaid, expert weather vane, adapter sublime, internalized it too well.

Difficulty. Oh, yeah. Difficulty spilleth over.

You always said to get out of Dodge, she telegraphs her late husband silently, fiercely, from under her blanket. *So I did. Get kicked around a little, you loved to say. Do you good. And because it actually seemed like a swell idea at the time, a magnanimous idea, I dragged your basset hound travel partner, Our Lady of Perpetual Sorrows, every agonized step.*

What a mothering fuck of lesson.

Ever since we landed, he's been in pain. Not simple pain. Not excise-able, mollifiable pain. It is throttled. Riven. Billy Budd pain. Pain of sheer perception. Pain of being. Pain of need. Refined, excruciating, insatiable as the Blob's, my darling. More than I could have dreamed—but thinking back, of course there was every evidence for it. He'd told me about fearing travel—but I thought he meant lousy destinations, second and third world shit-holes. He almost backed out just before we left but I blew that off, figured it for stage fright. He's always been gaga for the language; I was counting on that—once he was plonked into the setting I thought he'd take to it, sail along like a baby duck. My head so deeply up my ass, Kirk. What was I thinking? Sweetheart, I wasn't thinking. I was believing. A story I told myself, some Disneyfied fantasy. In the day to day? Every gesture, every move requires plotting like war generals, followed by a vote. If he loses, he sulks. Marcel Marceau doing Sad. Which café. Which grocer. I have said nothing about the sleeping mask and earplugs, the twenty-five minutes of nightly dental cleaning with exotic instruments, the swallowing of eyedropperfuls of herbal tincture at bedtime (head tilted back, like taking communion). Nor do I mention the hand sanitizer applied hundreds of times a day, also to doorknobs, faucets, handles. The bed (his bed) must be carefully made before we exit a room. Shoes lined up like little soldiers. Christ help us if he doesn't beg for a second pillow at every hotel, even though the French don't really do pillows, remember.

When his needs don't get met, he's wounded. He retreats. And if I don't rush in with the Band-Aids, suffering intensifies. Comes off him in waves, like a powerful smell. Sometimes I stop rushing in—a little sadistically, just to see what'll happen. But it backfires, because I am the sole recipient of his angst. Like standing under a bucket of warm tar. Of course you would argue I should split off from our pal. Except I can't, sweetie; the rooms are booked; budget's tight. We can go different ways for a morning or day and we do that sometimes, but I've got to live with him until we're done with this, and I don't want to rip the poor sod's heart out. So on we stagger through a world of choices, my dearest, each more freighted than the last. The light coat or the heavier coat? Salade or plat du jour? Why is the Listerine here not the same as the Listerine at home? Hunting down, first thing in any town, not the Roman ruins or the Picasso-Cezanne exhibit but the nearest laverie—the man's obsessed with laundromats. Which direction to walk, which carnet of tickets gives the best deal, what time we should eat, where to eat—which goddamn table. Crises, crises all. It's as if—and I have thought this through, my love—it's as if there were some golden uber-experience to be had out there, like Ali Baba's cave. And all these elements, the food, the sights, the fucking position of a table—the minutiae of going about it—if we nail these particulars exactly right, like clicking the correct numbers on a safe's dial, they'll open the cave door, the comme il faut door. And my task, holy God help me, is to enable that.

Didn't it always used to be me who took this rap? The way you used to storm at me for fussing? Dearest, I look like a Green Beret next to our Ollie.

Whenever I wonder how you handled this man in Mexico, my sinking chest gives the answer: He deferred to you. You were the alpha. But here, I'm the tailbone. Caboose.

Except that's not technically true. He'll do whatever I want. It's the dolorosa that weighs on me, sweetheart. He reminds me more and more, as you once said, of a Giacometti figure. Long tall stick-figure of sadness. Seeming to move, but not moving. Isolated, paralyzed, inconsolable. To be with him is to be forced to absorb it, carry it, respond to it—but there's the tyranny, darling. Response is disallowed. No one's permitted to address it let alone fix it—only to be dragged down by it, sagging under the suck burden. In this lovely country (putting aside weather) which is supposed to give us some fairly direct joie, the man spends his waking hours in a

stricken state, as though he'd been listening to too much Enya. All
of it conveyed without words. More like radio wave. Make that
microwave. It would be funny if it weren't such a world-class
ass-pain.

No wonder he can't find a new lover.

Oh, God. I'm sorry I said that, Kirk. I'm sad as anyone for his
loneliness. Sad as anyone for him losing Ennis the way he did.
Unbearable. Something conspiratorial about it. As if the man
weren't damaged enough—

She closes her eyes trying not to re-imagine the scene, though
it pops forward like a bad driving school film: Ollie's phone call
that mild October day, a Saturday, his shredded voice unnatu-
rally high, *Ennis is dead;* she'd stuffed a few things into a bag and
jumped into her car and flown that car (miraculous no cop
stopped her) down the 101 she hates to drive, to his apartment.
He'd buzzed her in; she'd taken the stairs two at a time and found
him doubled over on his couch like he was puking (he had
indeed vomited earlier). She'd bent to wrap her torso and arms
over the weeping man as if to protect his hunched form. His
arms and neck cool, covered with goosebumps, and he smelled
like toothpaste from scrubbing out his mouth after puking.
Opera was still playing on his FM, a man and woman in rapid
back-and-forth, the sort of passage that sounds inane even in
Italian. She rushed to the tuner and switched it off. He'd learned
of the crash by accident, surfing the *Chronicle* online that morning. One of those small subheads, and it was only the place name
that had drawn Ollie's eye: *Two Bay Area Men Die in Palm*
Springs Crash. The car, an ice-blue Porsche belonging to the
older man, the one who owned the Forestville property, had
been totaled. The roads connecting those desert cities (Fran
knew from visiting with Kirk) are dry and straight, surely
tempting to a driver whose vehicle is a pristine speed machine.

And when the driver has money to buy anything, Fran was thinking bitterly—including a boy at his side who looks like Colin Farrell—he surely feels invincible. But when she went to the computer to read the piece, still onscreen under Ollie's screen saver (the famous old woodcut of a man poking his head through heaven to view the workings of the cosmos), she'd learned it was Ennis who'd been at the wheel.

> PALM SPRINGS, Calif. (AP)—Two men, both Bay Area residents, were killed when the Porsche Boxster they were driving careened off the road, rolling several times before crashing into a rocky outcropping several hundred feet from the highway.
>
> Riverside County coroner's officials say 52-year-old Adrian Fleischer, scion of San Francisco's philanthropic Fleischer family, and 35-year-old Ennis Carmody, a Sonoma County landscape gardener, were in all probability killed instantly when the vehicle, registered to Fleischer, struck the rocks. It took emergency crews an hour to retrieve the bodies from the wreckage; the two men were pronounced dead at the scene.
>
> The Riverside County Register reported that two eyewitnesses observed the car moving at tremendous speed when it lost control.
>
> Rescuers noted that Carmody had been driving.
>
> Fleischer was a familiar name to fundraisers for the San Francisco arts, including ballet, opera, and several prominent museums, annually donating substantial sums to these causes, in keeping with his family's long tradition.
>
> Carmody provided landscaping services for several Bay Area private schools, and for private homes in both San Francisco and Forestville.

No photographs appeared with the webpage article.

She made Ollie talk to her. He hadn't heard from Ennis, it seemed, since summer's end, and grown more worried when Ennis had not answered his calls: again and again Ollie heard the gruff recording, *Ennis here, back to you when I can. Cheers.* When Ollie tried, using information in the paper, to phone the family to learn whether he might attend any sort of memorial, a frosty female voice, older, patrician accent, cut him off. Who were you to Ennis, the voice demanded.

Ollie stammered, astonished.

I—I'm—a good friend. I was—a close friend.

No, stated the voice. As if it already knew, and condemned, what Ollie had been. That will not be possible. Family only.

Ollie resumed weeping, and Fran wept with him.

Then she took him outdoors, walking slowly, holding his arm with both her hands, very much as he had done with her four years earlier. The day was typical, cool, cloudy. They hobbled to Stow Lake, watched the paddleboats and ducks on the filthy water. On the way back she bought groceries from Andronico's, still keeping hold of one of his arms. Once back she fixed them both double bloody Marys; ordered Chinese food. They ate chow fun and black bean chicken and watched television, a documentary about Antarctic wildlife—ideal because it was barren, hard: scoured of human imprint, at the edge of the world. She made herself a bed on his couch. Before she put him to bed, she read aloud to him. She knew Ollie liked her voice and she loved reading aloud, though Kirk had rarely had patience for it. She found a copy of *Great Expectations* on Ollie's shelf, flumped onto her belly across the bottom of his bed like a dog while he lay beneath his covers, eyes closed; from her end of the bed she saw only nostrils and cheekbones. *My father's family name being Pirrip, and my Christian name Philip, my infant tongue could make of both names nothing longer or more explicit than Pip.* Ollie listened. She'd had the wits to remember to bring some of her Ambien; she gave him two and herself one to swallow that night, and before she left the next day she wrapped several more for him in Saran Wrap. No funny business with these now, she'd warned at his front door before turning to leave, pressing the crumpled plastic wad into his hand, looking up at him. It was always difficult not to feel like a little kid standing before him, because of his height. He'd stared down at her in a trance. Yet somewhere in that face she saw, or felt, his affection. Adding to that his basic timidity—this time she thanked God for it—reassured her. He wouldn't try to off himself.

She is sober now under her bedclothes.

Though sometimes, sweetheart—I think it may have been far more cruel for both of them if Ennis had been murdered by AIDS. But it's absurd to speculate that way. Obscene. Of course I don't say anything about such thinking to Ollie. There'd be no chance for it anyway. He won't talk about it.

But I see men cruising Ollie, sizing him up. And I urge him every chance I get to go—go scouting. He won't. And again, he won't talk about it.

Her hands, under the blanket, scrinch up handfuls of bottom sheet.

How will he meet anyone? How can he even say ciao when he's so strangled?

She opens her hands, presses them, splayed, against the mattress.

Sweetheart, I've no heart to square off with the poor dude. What can it serve? Nothing will come of it but more grief. He'll pull in deeper, take it as another betrayal from someone he trusted, another blow. He'll turn all Russian on me.

Not that that would represent a grand departure.

An exhale escapes her.

Of course his having the language helps worlds. It's so touching, honey, to see him light up when people notice. He carries a pocket dictionary everywhere, insists on stopping to look up anything he doesn't recognize, traffic signs, labels, banners in store windows, marquees, those tiny blackboards in the windows of brasseries where they scrawl the day's specials. It gets irritating—you're walking along talking and suddenly you notice you're talking to air: he's stopped dead two blocks back, flipping furiously through his dictionary. If he can't find the word he needs his face grows dark, and I know he is cursing the dictionary's makers for their shoddiness, which in turn will remind him of the doomed state of the universe, and then everything will go straight down the toilet unless I start to sing and dance.

It gets better at cocktail hour, when we've had a few. The alcohol seems to cut a wire that was binding him like a newspaper bundle; I can see his whole being let down. Then for a while we do relax. We have something like what I dreamed of when I proposed this escapade. Short-lived, though. And the wine's weak here—at least the kind we can afford. Beer doesn't work. It's pleasant but mainly colored water, and then you have to pee more, meaning deal with the toilets. I should start carting bottles of gin in my bags. Seriously, sweetie, I'm going to compile a portable bar. I know you'd approve.

Well, first you'd laugh. And I'd deserve it.

She hears bedclothes stir, hears Ollie enter the bathroom and softly shut the door. She hears his battery-powered toothbrush fire up, a sonic whine like a small weed-eater.

She throws off the blankets, sees the rain flinging itself against the rectangle of glass.

She groans aloud, pulls the bedclothes back over her head.

This is it, this is it, this is it!

Fran seizes the rail of the balcony, a narrow overlook on the rue Jules César; she leans out, hopping in place two or three times like a child—as though (he muses) she is gazing from the deck of a gigantic ship while it slowly slides from port. The air is cold and damp, sky a grimy cotton. Chilled wind floods the room; the curtains, a babyshit-colored chintz, balloon and ripple. Below her, cars and motorcycles push in every direction, their constant revving peppered with shouts from the street. And behind and above this, the white-noise roar reverberating their bodies and bones, his and Fran's, through walls and glass and furniture, splendid terrifying thrum of the great sleepless engine of the city. The centerpiece of their balcony view, directly across the street, is a pornography store: three X's the whole of its title. She turns to face Ollie; he watches from a wooden chair in the shadowed end of the room, his long legs crossed, plastic cup of champagne in his hand. They'd picked up the cheap bottle, not even cold, from the *épicier* a few doors down—the same guy Fran remembers being there ten years earlier.

Their room and its appurtenances, except for the babyshit curtains, are bright orange. Street-roar, car horns, cold air swirl in. Fran talks half at him, half at the view, so he has to crane forward to hear.

The Bastille is the *zone,* Ollie. The best place to be. This used to be our hood, our beat. There's a tiny street just a few blocks from here, Rue Crémieux, I'll take you there right away—like a piece of another century, enchanted—and a little movie house past the new opera—they play strange, fabulous stuff there—and the most wonderful restaurant; I can't wait to show you—and the mussels place—and you see how close it all is to the Gare—Kirk loved this hood; he knew everything, everything.

Ah God, how I wish—

Her face, so full of light, suddenly drains, crumples.

He is out of the chair in a bound, bending to place his hand on her arm. She lowers her head. He squats close to look up into her face.

Frannie. Yes, I know. But think, think how it would please him that we got here. Wouldn't it just—Ollie rakes his memory for language, grabs the nearest fool phrase—wouldn't it just *make his day?*

She and Kirk had deep history here. Many visits: some as part of his teaching semesters. In her mind, since Kirk's death, that history has likely taken on a halo—by now she'll have easily forgotten the clashes, the angers, anxieties, exhaustion. Ollie had feared, during their planning, that it might hurt her terribly to see this city again. And during all their back-and-forths he'd suggested this to her many times, point blank. Each time she'd brushed it aside with a bravado he'd suspected was forced.

I'll invent a new way to be there, she'd written back airily. Her tone, at least onscreen, seemed to insist that some sort of practical grace would fall from the sky when time came for it. Bad bet. But then the whole venture—but never mind. Too late for that.

Her closed face still turns away. He takes her cold hands, cocks his own face this way and that, trying to catch her eyes.

Yes? We made it, Fran. All your doing. Full credit. Here we are. *Nous voilà.* Thanks to you. And it's not over yet, my dear. Eh? Best yet to come. *Grace à toi.* Yes, Frannie?

He is frightened she will cry. He dreads, as usual, not having the right words—whatever it takes to soothe her. He, who's tended thousands of wailing toddlers in every state of crackup. But there was always something he knew he could do to jolly the kids, some trick or distraction. Bursting into song often made a difference. *Alouette, gentille Alouette* he'd bellow, squatted beside them, rocking right and left singing while he busied himself cleaning the wound or blotting up tears, snot, paint, gravel. And their wet eyes would pop wide and their pouting mouths turn slyly upward, regarding the gangly singing man with new awe. As if he had just whispered the best joke of all time into their ears. With Fran he can't find any jokes, let alone wisdom. He carries no arguments against loss, against its finality—none that wouldn't sound like psychobabble.

She gazes at him now, from far away. Yeah, she finally says. She thinks a moment, not seeing him. Then she pats him on the cheek absently and turns back toward the whipping air of the street, squinting into the overcast light, pressing her lips tight.

They are both tired, as is always true after the rising and bathing and driving and hiking and interrogating and ticketing and hauling of selves and luggage. They'd succeeded, miraculously, in finding the Toulouse rental car station, buried in a compli-

cated warren of offices and parking lots, where they'd said good-
bye to the car. He'd driven them to the site, and then she'd leapt
from the vehicle and made arm movements like a signalman to
guide him through the maze of guard-poles and security gates.
In part to conserve energy, in part as damage control, they have
learned to say only what is necessary. Even when things go well
they remain quiet: sitting opposite each other on the *Très Grande
Vitesse* from Toulouse, the trains now familiar enough to be
consoling, bags of food and plastic bottles of water and unopened
magazines to hand, each of them staring out a window. Ollie
loves the trains, especially the *TGV*. Once you climb on and
dump your bags the armor can fall off: no effort needed, no
movement or speech as one is whished along, free to dream of
nothing, fill one's eyes with emerald land, sunflowers, farm-
houses and castles, grazing white cows ribboning past. It sur-
prises him, sitting in the hurtling car, the steady vibration
beneath him, to feel the whole structure of his obsessions, like
a wallful of clanking medals, evaporate against that fleeing
backdrop: he has trouble, in these blurred ligaments of time,
recalling details of his own life, blank and entranced in a carful
of brooding passengers—babies and children, mothers, com-
muters, *grandmères,* teenagers whose ears are corked with the
hiss of iPod music. If he hadn't visited some of those small ocher
kingdoms flying past (snugged into the seams of hills or crown-
ing them, turrets and steeples and crenellated ramparts like
golden pie-crust) he'd view them as fairy tales. But he knows
more now about the cost of that beauty, the foolishness of trying
to enter or appropriate it; air impenetrable, distilled over centuries. Yet as a framework for dreams it still works well, and maybe
because of that, flows too quickly—morphing too soon into
sooty industrial outskirts that give way at last to the sprawling

hub, the Gare de Lyon, a seething heaving organ, breathing people in and out of itself—flushing them out and sucking them back in all day and night.

Let's get out there, Ollie, Fran says softly.

Like kids, they doubletime it down the dark stairwell, each step scarcely wide enough for a single body. The clerk is the same bored, shrugging Pakistani clerk; the lobby television's blue screen blithers the same staccato talk-show jabber—handsome middle-aged men and women perched on stools around a kidney-shaped countertop straight out of the fifties, joking and quipping at speeds far beyond him. The stained red carpeting—its imperceptible design—the narrow spiral staircase smelling of disinfectant, dirty sheets piled outside the doors behind which *les bonnes,* tired African women, move heavily, the hopeless elevator, size of a coffin, rattling and wheezing up and down in cartoonlike torpor: all is as Fran remembers it, and this is part of her joy, and her anguish. Especially, it seems, the light: a pearling gray that bathes every surface with ruthless uniformity, like a coating of ash. The result is a patina both heightened and tender, ancient, muting other colors. Like the milky old daguerrotypes, Nadar's work. Grass, stone, and water will appear as they did millennia ago, and despite the chaos of rap music and op-art furniture and Galerie Lafayette and Starbucks and cellphone stores, again and again the modern trappings will go transparent and Ollie will teeter with the sense of having dropped back hundreds of years: if he narrows his eyes he will easily see (and smell and hear) clopping horses, wood-wheeled carriages, women with cinched waists and *chapeaux,* bustles and parasols—and further back, rags and street barricades and corpses, and back further still to plodding oxen and water carriers, shatterbelts of villages, greasy smoke, naked children, gypsy tribes. He will catch intermittent whiffs of sewage, unsure of its source, sulphurousness like offal from a cached monster, centuries in it, a thrilling stink. All this will converge with the roar. It will feel like nothing else, anywhere. His senses will buckle.

They push one after the other through heavy glass doors, emerge from the crowded, cleaning-fluid-smelling lobby out onto the dirty cement, the cars, the smack of cold, pearling gray.

She leads him around like a slave. Or rather, he functions as her bodyguard. He follows just a beat behind her, a tall shadow. They march to the Place des Vosges, through the shadowy arched entry into the pale sunlight of the square: a time-travel portal. Once through, they stop and stare. Sounds issue at them: splashing water from the fountain, echoes from the cool arcades surrounding the lawn, the demure trees: chatter, music, scents of coffee and roasting meats and fresh bread and perfume, laughter. Couples strewn on the grass, entwined, twirling strands of each other's hair; mothers and nannies trail young charges who lurch around shrieking, arms in the air, just as they do at the park at home. *Plus ça change,* he murmurs to Fran. She nods, her face in a kind of clench; he glances again and sees she is weeping soundlessly. An ensemble, two young men and a woman, accordian, guitar, and bass, arranged in the nearest arcade corner, are playing Astor Piazolla and they are very good; the stone archway's acoustics first-rate. Fran stands next to him, arms folded tight, two wide glistening paths down her cheeks, face clamped; she keeps untangling a hand to press away cascading water, retwining her arms.

He's given up his alarm. He must accept that Fran will be weeping a lot, at least for this portion of things. He doesn't say anything, or move to touch her. Kirk or no Kirk, he can't blame her. The laughing people, the movement, music and light—dailiness like a gentle carnival, some sort of sweeter, smarter world, playing out against seventeenth-century brick and stone.

He's made at once childlike and old in this place. The morning smell of grass, damp stone.

She leads him into the Marais.

Why aren't we talking about sex, Ollie?

She tosses back the last of her *pression,* strings of beer foam lining the glass. They are having a sit-down, as Kirk used to term it, outside a glassed-in café on a busy corner of the Marais, an oyster-colored disk of sun muffled behind the overcast. It's humid and cool, chestnut leaves riffling along the boulevards like soft green fans. They have walked until their legs feel like boards, past edifices of flesh-colored stone with twenty-foot-tall doors and phantasm handles—a human hand or grimacing face or chimera—past Turkish rugs, bead jewelry, scarves, temples and (as they ventured onto the Rue St. Antoine) cathedrals, displays of food in cramped shop windows. Fran has stopped weeping, for the present. They've walked the entire Pont des Arts, marveled at flora, dogs—yes, the leaky-eyed rat-sized sort, trembling in handbags—citizens on benches eating lunch. He and Fran have fantasized aloud, gaily, about owning any single one of the charming apartments lining the flowered path. Looping back, they've paused again in the Marais. Lines of tourists eddy through the passageways, snaking in and out of the *haute-haute* boutiques (items of clothing displayed like rare manuscripts), a moving forest of white legs and running shoes, eating falafel sandwiches and gyros and ice cream, camera gear swinging, babies peering from carriages and chestpacks, kids yelling. There is no end to the flow, the walkways too narrow to bear the crowds: they spill into the street, scatter and regroup, dodging cars and minibikes, edging between parked vehicles, shouting in many languages. He can't help thinking of the necklace of characters stumbling along the ridgetop, as if stuck together, in *The Seventh Seal.* Was one of them carrying a goose?

Though Fran's question has startled him and as usual, tightened his heart—why, why does everything she asks seem to imply some rank failing of his?—he's so sick of this reflex, of his own cravenness, that he pushes it aside the way he'd wave away a bee. Three Ricards on an empty stomach have made him bold, the licorice aftertaste still agreeable on his tongue. He regards her evenly, though he's aware his heart rate has clotted.

Why is it necessary, he asks.

She scans the crowds, burps softly against her palm. She wears her money and credit cards in a small flat pouch strung from a cord around her neck, the oblong shape poking up under her blue T-shirt. A good blue for her, he thinks, half-shutting an eye. Close to delft. She should wear it more. Something to consider. *One has time,* he decides, pleased to hear these words surface in the placid lake of his mind. Instructive. No matter where one is. Time has accordioned open, helped by alcohol. Beyond their sight, someone's begun playing jazz clarinet. The tune—bizarrely—is "Someone to Watch Over Me."

Too bad we're not a film, Ollie thinks dreamily. A film we

could walk out on, just at this shot. The credits could start roll-ing right now.

Because, Fran is answering, I worry we're avoiding the obvious.

What's obvious? He toys with his empty tumbler; adding:

Do you think Jane Fonda talks about her sex life a lot these days?

Fran raises her brows, amused and faintly surprised.

Hey. Immaterial, Your Honor.

Why immaterial? She's not that much older than we are.

He is wearing the white baseball cap she bought him, that reads *Legion Étrangère: Marche ou Crève* in black letters above the tricolored stitching on the front. He tugs the bill lower and leans back—as best he can in the dollhouse-sized chair.

I mean why shouldn't we talk about it, Fran says, folding her arms, her eyes still traveling the passing caravans. You haven't been with anyone since Ennis, and that was—

Fran, dear.

His smile is forbearing. *One has time.*

Dear, it's demeaning to have to unpack this again. I don't wave the subject around in *your* face, do I?

She frowns. My case is different.

(He knows she means: *I had sixteen wholesome years, you've had kinky crumbs.*)

I want you to meet someone, she says. What's wrong with that?

All that's missing, he thinks, is for her to stamp her pretty foot. Fiddle-dee-dee.

He places folded hands on the table. *I am Reason's voice,* he thinks. *A United Nations dignitary in dashiki and baseball cap.*

Frannie, that's thoughtful, and I appreciate it. I really do. And from time to time, I admit, I wouldn't mind some companionship. But the sex, despite what you may believe, isn't the part that matters so much now. Can we agree to let it stand there, for simplicity's sake? For dignity's sake?

His hands feel chilly. He absolutely will not talk to her about the men he is noticing, or those who notice him, whose after-images he tries to banish. It is not for her to know, not for anyone to know, about the dreams these men inspire (however fleetingly). What he's just told her, anyway, is not far from true. He rarely masturbates anymore. The flame burns low—barely a pilot light. In any case he wants to check her at this habit, this proprietary bossiness. *Insupportable*—he adores the French word. Unbearable, her fix-it impulse. So American, even to another American. Very little, he now recognizes, is solvable: very little ever was, and that's the crucial news of aging, which (he begins to understand) if you simply grasp in a certain way can actually give real comfort. You just step back a step, he thinks, letting his eyelids half close. And at once, something loosens behind your temples. Was this the same thing as collapsing, curling into a dried-up ball? *Mais non, pas du tout.* More a subtle adjustment, like clicking into very low gear on an expensive bike.

So what about you? he says too loudly.

She shrugs. I don't seem to want sex anymore. I don't tell anyone that, but who's asking?

She smiles, leaning forward to pat his laced hands: Besides you, sweetie.

She settles back, pushing a curl behind her ear. I don't mind it. I remember sex with Kirk of course, always lovely, and it makes me sad. Well, sad and happy. Happy we had it. I loved being close to him, loved the smell of him—

She pauses, biting a lip. She waits a moment.

But the thing is, she says. After some time, after Kirk died, I came to feel relieved to be done with it. And I sense that's not something you're ever supposed to say. I see the surveys—God, relentless. Old people can have hottie sex right up to the end, yeah, yeah. A kind of cheerleading. The culture's terrified, sweetie. Terrified of the end of sex. The end of sex means the end of selling, for American purposes. The culture can't think past that.

A glum, dusty man with black hair and olive skin appears beside the table, thrusting a bunch of long-stemmed roses into the airspace between Ollie and Fran, over their empty glasses. Had the man been smiling, he might have resembled an underweight version of the organ grinder depicted in old children's books. But there is no smile, and he won't meet their eyes. The tired bouquet hovers before their eyes like a small alien craft. The man's fingernails, Ollie can't help noticing, are rimmed with black grime. Ollie shakes his head. *Non, merci.* The flowerseller's face is an inert mask. He doesn't move or look at either of them, as if within this silent pause a change of heart may reasonably be expected. For a wretched instant Ollie wonders whether that's true—whether waiting a beat has succeeded for the man in the past. Ollie repeats his refusal, shaking his head more emphatically. The man's face never alters as he floats to the next table.

Disquieted, they sit a moment.

Fran resumes.

So—um. Right. I love the freedom now, of—of being invisible. Most men do not see me anymore, and Ollie, I can't tell you the anguish that saves.

She pauses.

Anguish may seem a strong word. I'm not claiming to've been a big beauty. It wasn't about beauty. Just the whole fucking mandate, the animal stuff. I couldn't walk along a sidewalk, most of my younger years, without getting harrassed. I mean I liked sex fine, coming of age. I always liked it; had lovers, adventures. They were innocent, untoxic.

Even in Africa? he wonders.

Sure. My group was so young. We were children, really. Romantic fools. Sometimes older men leered at us but there wasn't any—threat to it. Locals were too preoccupied staying alive.

She thinks a minute. But here—I mean in the States—the dues were always tough. There was a certain amount of pride, of course. I remember being able to walk into a room and feel men's eyes on me. That was a pleasure, I admit, bound up with vanity. But at the same time, I couldn't go running without it becoming an obstacle course—my shoulders always braced against the next chorus of screams, the car horns making me jump. I couldn't stand at a crosswalk and wait for a light to change without being—well, spattered, I guess. Noises, gestures. Invitations to sit on faces.

She sighs. What always fried me was that it almost never worked in reverse, at least not in the worlds I came up in. Young women didn't act that way, as a rule. Jesus. She shakes her head. I remember one guy coming straight at me and grabbing both my breasts with both hands before whizzing past, disappearing. Another time I remember some guy murmuring—the exact moment I passed him, Kirk walking right beside me— murmuring just low enough so that only I could hear, *breasts breasts breasts*. When I stopped and turned, staring after the guy in amazement, Kirk was saying *What's the matter? What happened?*

Her eyes survey the crowd. It's not like I ever got raped or molested or anything like that, thank God, thank God. But the tension, the targeted feeling. I often assumed there must have been something both comic and despicable about my appearance, about the way I presented in the world, and that somehow that was my fault. Something about me that drew mocking, drew catcalls. Anyway it never stopped, in one form or another, until, oh, my forties. And honestly, Ollie, I was overweight a lot of those years, a good fifteen pounds. Zaftig. Probably gave me ample breast tissue. Maybe that was the comic-despicable part. The tabloid image. But my breasts weren't extraordinary, I promise. They were unremarkable. See, it wasn't just me, I finally figured out. It was any young woman. Men were—oh, Ollie. It made me understand early on why women would turn to each other.

But then again I can see that somehow men, on their end of it, felt maddened. Shish-kebabbed. Not fair to them, either.

She leans toward him again, taps the table. Ollie, I remember seeing a movie theater empty out one night after the movie *Ten,* with Bo Derek. This was a million years ago, of course. But the faces of those men I saw coming out of that theater that night—oh, man. I can never forget it.

Their faces were dull and sick and blind. With rage, and with lust. Ready to murder someone. Worse.

She props a cheekbone against a fist, eyeing him. Depressing, huh? Even in past tense. I'm not sure, to tell you the truth, what it's like for young women now. Maybe it's fabulous. Everything I get is hearsay, women in the locker room, their daughters. Those girls are privileged, of course, smart, powerful. Actually, a lot of them are spoiled witless. But the good part of that would be, it helps them not take the same kind of shit anymore. You never know. I hope it's true.

His lovely Ricard buzz has evaporated; in its stead he feels vaguely penitent.

Fran, I'm sorry.

The men she speaks of are not men he's spent any time near or remembers noticing—never trained to notice, perhaps. Not since getting taunted as a kid. He'd become an early expert, despite his height, at hiding, going beige, blending into backdrops. Although, even tucked into the sheltering Bay Area most of his adult life, he's had his share of horror at the news, stories that float back. Murders, vendettas. Terror when AIDS swept the planet, a black plague time, grief for friends taken, swaths of them cut down like scythed crops, grief for the inconsolable partners they left. The city in a state of siege, for years. For years he kept two funeral suits in his closet, and his address books—he'd started several fresh ones—filled with scribbled black cross-outs. He avoided bathhouses, which were closing fast then anyway, but also, because of fear and shyness, avoided the clubs, glory-holing, amyl nitrate. Group gropes, high life—outside his orbit. The risks he took were minimal, infinitely more private. He took the tests early, and by some spittle-thread of grace escaped a positive reading. Ennis had claimed to have tested negative. Ollie went back for retesting after Ennis died, and felt limp when he received the same relieving news. He's kept himself doubly buffered since, resulting in no real understanding of gay *or* hetero high life.

Gently, he reminds her of this.

I know that, Ollie. In a way it worked out well for you. It protected you, even accidentally. Anyhow, now I can feel spared, too. It's heaven, being free of all that. I can walk around—if I do it in reasonable areas—without that horrible guardedness. I can transact business without having to pretend not to notice smirks and double entendres.

He's aware that something has also surely been lost to her in this switch, but knows better than to blurt it directly.

He tries a quieter tack.

Do you miss anything? Do you miss—flirting?

She makes a face. Not really. I've asked myself that. Flirting seems to've walked away by itself one day, just flat-out disappeared from the tool kit. The only time a man looks at me in a flirty way it's one of those ninety-year-olds at the gym, bless their dear souls. It puts extra blood in their cheeks if I smile at them, say a word or two back to them.

She thinks a moment. It sort of kills me when that happens, because I don't feel so far from them these days. From who they are. They don't quite seem the cartoon they once did.

She leans toward him, makes her voice low.

Remember how, when we were young, we thought the old were *born old?*

He nods, smiling weakly, rolls his eyes. He thinks of the barbershop.

She nods, sitting back. So I understand better how that conveyor belt's sailing along. I'm right behind those guys on it. Once in a while some duffer somewhere calls me *young lady*— convinced it's the wittiest thing he ever uttered. And then there's this awful stunned moment while it sinks in: I'm the punchline of that joke. My actual face. My *person.*

She looks hard at Ollie. Because I don't feel old. I don't feel like I have anything in common with people I consider old. You know this feeling, Ollie; I know you've had it.

He does. He has.

Frannie, might you please recall I asked you to promise you'd tell me when I started smelling that way?

She smiles. Yeah. That's right.

But you know? she says. After that bad moment, I laugh and beam at the guy who calls me *young lady* like he's a fucking genius.

Because it means I am safe.

Afternoon's darkening almost biblically: clouds thickened, low, buckling and metallic. Temperature's dropped; air smells of ions. Time to limp back to the room, bathe, pitch like felled trees onto their beds and (groaning) prop their feet against a wall, knees loose, let the blood reverse direction awhile before they haul themselves (groaning) back up to get dinner. It'll have to be the brasserie around the corner: impossible to walk any farther today. She'll order *poulet frites*. He'll have the same, or steak or *canard* if they have it. Whatever they eat will taste so good it will bring water to their eyes.

He rises; she stands with him. Brief dizziness. Their feet are bricks.

He searches his pocket; drops some coins on the table. The smallest piece, the copper *centime,* is the size of a child's pinky fingernail and as far as they can tell, useless.

Crowds have thinned. The clarinetist stops mid-phrase with an abrupt honk.

So Frannie, he says as the first hard drops *tink* against the metal table. If this safety you mention feels so good and is such a relief and all, why are you haranguing *me* about stepping up a sex life?

Cool ticks of water hit their arms and necks. They haven't thought, of course, to bring umbrellas. They thread faster along the narrow walk, through others pacing faster, scents of onions frying, perfume, dampened cement, car exhaust.

She waves an open hand as they scurry along. Because I worry. Because for a gay man I always assume the shelf life is longer—

She glances sharply at him.

I'm sorry. I meant that for a gay man, I figure the—um—the drive sticks around longer. That it's never too late.

The walkway grows narrower still. In a series of quick steps she scampers in front of him, turning her face to the side to throw words back at him.

Would I be wrong—she shouts sideways—assuming that?

He yells at the back of her head.

If Kirk could come back again somehow, would you want to have sex with him?

She stops so suddenly, whirling to face him, he almost runs her down.

Looks up at him, blinking against the peppering rain:

In a heartbeat, she says.

Now the droplets become a sheet, funneling down as if someone has overturned a bucket. Alongside everyone else they break into a run, and she tilts her head back and howls heavenward:

It's fucking *Auuuuguuhhst.*

The next day they spill from the black mouth of the Nation metro exit like ants from a teeming colony, across streets, across cement-and-grass islands, around dog walkers and baby carriages and crêpe stands, the mammoth cement wheel of Place de la Nation, making their ways (as if swimming) to a street off the Place, winding between business types in black suits, elderly couples, deliverymen hoisting crates from double-parked trucks.

Faces from old paintings, Ollie thinks. Rembrandts.

A morning of raw blue, overlaid by flanks of evenly spaced white rags of cloud—like those (glancing up, wincing at the stab to his temples) in the O'Keeffe painting.

He is hungover. Fran insisted on buying more booze from the little *épicier* on the way back from dinner. (*The same guy,* Fran couldn't stop marveling—though the Middle Eastern man crammed behind the counter showed not one particle of interest, except in the money they handed over.) She bought a bottle of

Côtes du Rhône, two tall cans of Kronenbourg 1664, a flask-sized Armagnac, a couple of apples, and a jar of wrinkled Greek olives. They toasted each other in the room. They toasted Kirk. They toasted history, they toasted France, the Marais, the Bastille, they toasted the miracle of air flight, the bravery of the immigrants who made the families who made them. They toasted every artist they could think of, living or dead, who'd been vigorous and productive late in life, and they toasted the hideous orange room and shit-colored curtains—its little television sizzling with the white-noise roar of soccer highlights.

He feels toxic. His eyes burn; his mouth tastes like mothballs, though he scoured his teeth twice this morning and used Listerine—knowing perfectly well this was making him take him even longer in the bathroom than usual but so engrossed, concentrating so deeply on his procedure that he jumped like a puppet, nearly capsizing the mouthwash bottle when Fran rapped hard, a furious staccato on the bathroom door.

He is certain French Listerine is a different substance from the American product. Inferior. Something odd in the flavor. Aftertaste metallic, not the same. Same for Dove soap—the scent is wrong, industrial. He would like to research this vexation, but knows he'll let it lapse after they leave.

They have three days left.

Loping along behind her in the cool air, his thoughts are dim and halting, coated with sticky webbing.

They pass the ebony wood facade and red-gold awnings of the wine franchise Nicolas, still closed at this hour—dear heaven, he doesn't even want to think about full, shiny bottles, let alone see them. They pass a raft of small *boucheries* and *charcuteries,* hooves and heads and cryptic animal parts redly arrayed, loaves and multicolored tarts and eclairs and almond cookies, proprietors sweeping water off sidewalks, students hurrying singly and in packs, smoking and smoking, old women beggars bent double speaking to their own ankles, shrouded so completely in black they seem to be a moving pile of black laundry, only the outstretched hand visible, twisted and quivering, mothy noises of entreaty from beneath the shroud, and children tethered to nannies and strollers, clasping a *pain au chocolat,* mouths smeared with chocolate and crumbs.

It's only morning, and their legs hurt.

Are you sure, he pants (she is walking fast) this was where it was.

Yes, she calls back without slowing. It's in this circle. Along this side. I'm sure. I remember the Casino market was not far from it.

She is pale, a trifle taut about the face, but otherwise unmauled by their mixed-drink festival of the previous night.

I want, he says between intakes of breath, to go into more of those little courtyards, like the ones we saw yesterday.

He likes the stopped-time feeling in these miniature parks, some half a block long, some just the triangular island between converging streets, their pigeon-shitted benches, many quite old, on a weekday morning. But the enclosed ones are best, walled on two or three sides by buildings. Unexpected, like a sudden idea. Sun-and-shade-checked; everyone away at work or school except a trickle of elders and clochards. Crumbling statuary, lumps of sculpture almost hidden by bushes. Little fenced beds, Peruvian lilies, pansies. Birdsong, especially from the merles, the blackbirds sleek with blue sheen, lifting and settling like flung fabric—music a chorus of glockenspiels. Doves, one or two, murmuring their sweet, sad inquiry: *c'est quoi, ça? c'est quoi, ça?* Sparrows hopping and swooping. The density of the patient earth, soaked with history like a liquored cake. Lord knows who sat or stood there, centuries ago. He likes imagining Rilke, Rodin. Walking canes, pocket watches on chains. He can search for the history of these little patches on Google anytime, of course, but he almost prefers not knowing. They carry a ruined air, especially mornings. It soothes him. A hole in time.

We can do that later, Fran is saying. I need your help with this.

Her legs going, going. Then with not one peep of warning she stops dead, and he nearly topples over her in his momentum.

We're close, she says, staring. I know we are.

They stand still on the walk, people and traffic flowing around them.

Her voice droops. I guess . . . maybe . . . maybe they closed. But things don't close that way here—or not so often as they do with us—

He waits alongside her, cars and crowds coursing past. She keeps turning, staring. Light splashes on chrome, hurting his eyes; he feels about in his jacket pocket for his sunglasses. Already the brasserie's sidewalk tables are filling; he can smell garlic steam, mussels. Then groping for the sunglasses he feels a boxy weight, the pleasant spritz of recollection: his dictionary. Happily, he closes his hand around it. It's always fun to look up some new provocation, especially menu items—

Fran cries out: There it is!

She takes off running, nearly struck by a taxi as she sprints across the street. The driver, an older man with silver hair whose face, Ollie can't help noting, resembles Federico Fellini's—is set in a kind of permanent disgust, as though his whole life has presented him with nothing but insults like this one—hits the horn. *Ahh, imbécile,* he groans, and there is a kind of pained satisfaction in his voice.

Ollie does his best to dart after her, trying to mark the doorway where she's disappeared, at the same time watching anxiously for a break in the inextinguishable press of cars.

A bookstore. Small front window, small overhead sign: *Marqu' Ta Page,* and beneath that, *Librairie.* A picture alongside: the final *e* in *Page* landed as if dropped, askew, into the middle of an opened book.

He pushes into the place and halts; after the chrome-blinding sun it takes his eyes a minute to adjust. But the smell—new paper, leather and moleskin, alcohol tang of highlighters and pens; glossy stock of trade covers—already gives immediate relief, the scent of asylum. At his left, facing the display window, a big writing desk covered with stacks of new books. In front of him Fran stands waiting, her eyes large and anxious. Beside Fran is the store's proprietress, a poised woman in her early forties, honey-colored hair pulled into a neat pony tail. She wears a sweater and straight skirt: the French, he has become convinced, don't even need to try to look as they do—attractive, thoughtful, self-possessed. Even in the quietest of either sex of almost any age, one whiffs a sheathed eroticism. *Tasteful* eroticism. Some sort of genetic given. Pregnant women are like goddesses here, like Roman statuary. (About the men he's less inclined to generalize, but certainly he admires their compactness, a compressed, seamless containment.) It's all terribly unfair, he and Fran have agreed. Fran has raved at him in despair about the perfection of French women—impossible skin, bone structure, effortless slenderness. *Gravity-free breasts,* she moans. It was—what is that word you like so much? Fran had demanded.

Insupportable, he'd answered.

Yeah. That.

Beyond Fran and the proprietress, the store plunges narrowly back like an overlarge train car, walls covered with packed shelves, tables bearing face-up titles the length of the passage, most of them trade paper, many the uniform Gallimard covers, alluring for their simplicity. He longs for time to inspect these at leisure.

No leisure available now, though.

Fran is vibrating like a stage mother.

Ollie, go ahead. Please tell this delightful woman what we talked about.

Ollie smiles apologetically at the woman, who waits with polite attention.

Dreadful to have to undertake this with a hangover, but he'd agreed to it merrily last night, full of enlarged purpose and (in the grip of three kinds of alcohol) new tenderness for his old friend. He draws a breath and begins, doing his best to sound logical and not screw up any conjugations.

Madame, my dear friend here used to live here in your neighborhood (*voisinage*)—very near this store (*de très très près*) as a matter of fact several years ago (*il y a quelques années*) with her late husband, who was a teacher. She and her late husband used to do their errands (*faisaient les cours*) in this area; they visited your store fairly frequently (*assez souvent*) and in front of your store they would often encounter (*rencontraient*) a big black dog, who was named Jazz (Ollie tries to give the z that tasty bit of ss at its finish). Jazz liked to sit out on the sidewalk and greet passersby (*les gens qui passaient*), and sometimes he would also be found (*se trouvait*) inside the store, but it was clear (*on a bien compris*) he belonged to the store. And my friend here—whose name is Fran, and my name is Oliver, by the way—my friend remembers she once came into your store during those years she lived here, in order to see Jazz, because she was by then very fond of him (*affectionée*), and was told the dog was on vacation for awhile in the south of France.

Ollie gathers another breath. Fran watches him, hands hooked tightly before her like she's about to sing an aria.

Madame, Ollie says. Is Jazz still here?

The sensible Madame speaks and moves with swift, unfussy grace.

But of course, monsieur, she answers in musical French, stepping over to the desk beside Ollie.

Jazz is sleeping here, she says, just under this desk.

At the desk she bends, speaking into the dark cave between the pillars of drawers on either side: the hollow where a seated human's legs would go if the desk had been used for writing.

Fran tilts forward, hands against her cheeks.

Do you hear, Jazz? Madame calls in French into the cave. We have a *gentille madame* who has traveled a long way (*qui est venue de très loin*)—she has come today just to see you again. Come say hello, please; show your manners.

Ollie translates this for Fran, who is now weeping uncontrollably.

And then out from the cave, to Ollie's astonishment, unfolds a big handsome black lab whose face bears a white chin: the white stretches up toward his ears as though the beard were strapped on, and the white streak flows downward, along his neck and chest. He looks up at his visitors equably, and his tail gives a couple of wide thwaps.

Ollie's speechless. Slowly, it occurs to him the animal must be accustomed to being summoned this way, to greet old fans.

Fran kneels, burying her face in the old dog's neck. He licks her hand.

Again, Ollie can't help wonder. Is this practiced? Choreographed?

Jazz. Fran's voice is breaking from deep inside his fur. Jazz, you're here. You're still here.

He is an older fellow now, the proprietress explains calmly to Ollie, as they look on. His energy is less; he naps a lot.

Ollie has pulled Fran's camera from the other pocket of his jacket (where it balances the weight of the dictionary) and pressed the button:

Fran's arms around the animal; her swollen, streaked, glad face. The black-furred celebrity: smiling, patient, genial.

Madame stands by, placid. Perhaps, indeed, this happens all the time. While they take turns thanking her, Jazz noses back into the dark desk-cave to resume his sleep.

S o let's review, she says to the dark lake water before them.

Reviewing was always Kirk's term. He loved going back over activities. Naming them let him re-live them, and thus, she guessed, have them twice. He loved lists.

Things we've seen, she prompts Ollie.

(Places she's dragged him.)

He makes no answer, watching the water. He smiles wanly.

Ichabod-Ollie.

She knows she will be gasping with relief to hug him good-bye. They go back together on the same flight, but (thank holy God) they don't sit together on that plane. She'll settle into her seat numb, voided, as if she's just shed two hundred pounds. Drag her case twelve hours later out into the glare of late morning at SFO, eyeballs burning, climb onto her northbound bus alone alone alone. (He'll take a city airporter.) She'll sleep on the bus like a passed-out drunk, curled up sideways on two seats, drooling on the flight bag serving as her pillow, until the driver taps her when they reach her stop. She'll stare out the taxicab window, not listening to the cabbie's radio baseball or his half-hearted talk about the recent heat wave. How intense the light—she'll have forgotten its intensity, the legacy of the northern half of the state—blazing yellow and pewter in it, and yet she will also be able to tell it's softened, diffuse, the light of waning summer. Another fall, with no Kirk to remark on the changing light. Clockwork, he was. Every year he loved to say it. They both loved to say it as they stared out at the Japanese maple.

The light's begun to do that thing it does.

And the air.

She'll enter the house and stare around in silence, bewildered by its scruffiness, trying to remember, to fix the shape in her mind, of what it had so long contained. A girlfriend once told her you had fifteen minutes to see your house as it really was, after you'd been away some time: its shabbiness, its funk. The same brief window of clarity, surely, applied to the life one had led before the travel. Stunned, she'll be, to resume days as a solitary agent. To look ahead to months of not-Ollie. Of not stepping around the careful mixing of his vitamin powder into a plastic cup of water every morning. No waiting twice a day for the time-sucking ceremonies in the bathroom. No sanitizer spray. No crucified face floating alongside her or across tables, a persistent visitation from a Bergman film.

But Ollie has never complained. Not aloud. She'll give him that. His face may be a road map of morose, his body a scarecrow's, but he's kept uncivil words unspoken. And he's agreed to all her wishes, all the rounds they've made. Trotted beside or just behind her, like one of those service dogs. Snapped photos of her and her beloved Jazz, of the *bouquiniste* sheds along the Seine, the golden angels trumpeting on the Pont Alexandre III—whatever she wanted.

God love the ghoul: she has given up any hope for whatever it was she hoped for him. But he's been, at least, amenable.

All of their stops an homage to Kirk, of course. A kind of Greatest Hits tour.

The Musée de la Vie Romantique, fetid, dusty. Vincennes— the castle, and a couple of big *salades* in town. The miniature Statue of Liberty in the Luxembourg. *Apéros* outside a corner bar on Rue Vavin, just off the gardens. The Suzanne Valadon exhibit at the Pinacothèque, along with a few canvases by her poor fucked-up kerosene-swilling son, Utrillo. Parc Monceau. La Mouffe. Slices of pizza with an egg baked onto them. Ollie climbed five flights of stairs at Gibert Jeune, inquiring at each level, to find his slender copy of Jean-Dominique Bauby's *Le Scaphandre et le Papillon*. The Cluny, its gray crypt light, made them somber; they resolved after that to stay above ground as much as possible. They walked Canal St. Martin, grungier than she remembered. Chez Paul—crazy-busy, snottier than before; she and Ollie backed out and traipsed down the street to eat cheap Asian instead. The D'Orsay. (Louvre lines too long, but they combed the gift shop downstairs.) Willy Ronis photographs in the Moneychangers building. Rivoli, its deathless glittering junk, its arid mannequins. The Aligré market where she and Kirk had always bought sublime *fougasse,* onions and mushrooms and potatoes in them. (It appalled her, and in the next minute seemed fitting, that the *boucherie* no longer makes the *fougasse*.) And up in Montmartre the Abbesses stop, the steep hidden streets, gimcrack stores.

Cité de la Musique, ugly as a Soviet concourse, where she'd bought some of her best CDs. And along the outside walls, shredded old posters for the socialist candidate, that woman with the hyphenated last name who always lost. The shop near Hôtel des Deux Continents, where she and Kirk found the tablecloth with the deep red poppies—red of garnets. Ollie wandered with her, both of them touching the delicate, expensive faience with a kind of terror. Both have now mastered the singsong *Bawjou'* as they enter each shop; both chime the same gliding *Merci au'voi'* as they exit. Politesse: a matter of mimicry. Frosty but lavish, like bowing low.

She recites all this to him.

Yes, he says from time to time, nodding as she itemizes. Yes, that's right.

She skips the part about escorting him down a couple of Marais streets lined with open-front gay bars, the handful of habitués regarding the passing world from barstools, eyes full of a certain bitter languor, like smoke from dry ice. (Ollie had grown very nervous.)

Today she's made him hike with her into the Bois de Boulogne; joggers and cyclists whizzing around, people on lunch break unwrapping sandwiches at the edge of the lake. Ducks. Willows. Algae-and-grass smells. Occasional cars purr along the drive behind them, but the wide sky, open air and canopying trees, the release from the cement labyrinth of the city, loosens something in them. It's breezy, clouds long and silvery. They sit on damp grass near the water, eating black grapes. Ollie's long legs, crossed at the ankle, seem to extend halfway down the bank.

A soundtrack for this, she thinks, could be Chopin's *Berceuse.* A lullaby.

Or Delius. That lilting piece about a river in Florida.

How are your feet? she asks presently.

He appears pleased. He loves to assess the shifting states of his body. She's hardly exempt. Of course their Rules forbid it publicly. But no harm in it, she guesses, between fellow prisoners out of earshot—in an alien language to boot.

Not bad, he says, leaning back, propped by his elbows, to watch the long boats of his feet, wagging them so they appear to be waving hello. He's worn the same shoes the entire trip, a style she sees everywhere: webbed sandals closed at the toe, soles of automobile tires, as if huaraches had mated with hiking shoes. He'd acquired them early from L. L. Bean to break them in. Not handsome, but practical. He's also brought moleskin and Band-Aids.

I broke them in pretty well before we left, Ollie says, still watching his feet as if for argument. Of course you can never know in advance how they'll perform. Yours?

Fine so far, she says, hugging her knees. She wears her favorite soft loafers, designed with eyelets for air. She'd found them in a store called Walkabye. Costly, even on sale, but worth it—no blisters. During the months of planning she loved reminding Ollie that the problem of travel shoes was insanely more difficult for women. You're supposed to carry just two pairs, one for going out, one for everything else, but it's hopeless: no pair is completely right and your feet change in transit, swollen all the time.

She doesn't mention the scab in the upper back of her left nostril that won't heal but feels tight and blocks the flow of air; that all her fingernails have cracked and torn, that her own feet have swollen, their soles red and inflamed, thicker callouses over the little toes, knobby beginnings of bunions more pronounced.

A perfect blue-black crescent underscores each of her eyes, as if the side of a teaspoon had been pressed hard into the tender pale tissue.

You know your feet change as you get older, she reminds him now, pointlessly. I read it in the AARP magazine. They get wider, and they swell.

Sounds realistic, he says, looking out again at the water.

Then he thinks of something, looks at her.

Do you happen to know—have you read—does your nose grow larger, too? As you age?

She frowns. No idea, she says. Haven't read anything. But I'll check it out.

He nods again.

A chain of cyclists hurtles across the bridge at the other end of the lake; their happy shouts echo back.

Strange, she says, leaning back on her elbows. I used to buy all my clothes and shoes from thrift shops in the city. Buffalo Exchange in the Haight, couple of others. Used to wear high heels to work every day like it was nothing, absolutely nothing. And at that time, it *was* nothing. Made not a grain of difference. And you know what I'd have for breakfast when I was under-slept, and hung over? A cup of triple-strength black coffee chased by a Diet Coke. Instant fix.

Mmm. Ollie stares at the water.

Now every choice, she says, has so much—moral weight, for Christ's sake. Even the choice to *ignore* the moral weight has moral weight.

True, he says.

But he's not with her; he is drifting, talked out.

They have one full day left. The day after that they fly home.

They sit watching the water, the silver light.

Time, she thinks, feels un-striated here.

Of course they're vacationers. The quality of time's been rented. A temporary trick. But the movements of others remind them of dailiness, chores, obligations. Lives lived against dead-lines, consulting watches. Just like their American counterparts. Defined, declared, in motion. All of it urgent, all of it stressed, of course. Pressé, Ollie would say.

As if living, she muses, were a partisan act. A bunch of patriots hiding out in the hills, sitting around campfires at night with hungry eyes and soot-streaked cheeks.

But no, not really. Living's a default mode—until trauma. Some horrible ordeal. Then you have to *choose* it.

And re-choose it. Boy, do you ever. Again and again. Like one of those machines pitching tennis balls at you, fast. Swatting and swatting.

She'd had several close encounters with the morpheus sirens, of course. Considered gathering up all the pills—leftover prescriptions, sedatives, sleeping pills. There were plenty of them, more than enough to do the job. Something in her always balked before she could follow the idea too far. A reflex, like gagging. It was going to happen anyway: why not use up whatever life remained, just to see what would happen?

But what exactly, she wonders now, are we going back to?

She sits forward, rubbing the long grass from her elbows: crisscrossed red indents where the grass has pressed in.

She's worn, like Ollie. Scrubbed out. Too sapped even to send bulletins to Kirk. As plain as anything, *it's harder to do this because we're older.*

They tire more easily—can't walk as far as they thought they could. They crave naps even if they forgo them, and forgoing naps gives a thin, burnt quality to perception, a not-enough-air tightness through the rest of the day. When stores or ticket offices are closed, or some vital entity goes on strike (constantly, it seems)—the blow feels deliberate, even conspiratorial—the aggravation violent. Hunger arrives in a sudden, crucial cramp, and there's no waiting around to eat the way they both once might have. She used to scorn Ollie for this—now finds she too gets shaky, a bit dizzy, if food is not found at once.

Automatically she reaches into the damp paper bag, on the

grass between them, for more grapes. Mostly a mess of broken stems.

Still. It was not wrong, she thinks, to do this trip.

Ollie's insane, but that was never exactly a revelation, so she can't count it as a misfire. *Travel beats the living shit out of you.* That part she'd truly underestimated. Every day's a world, an assault. You gear up each morning to take it on. At some level, that fact is always known—but it's not a thing you cared to dwell on in the planning.

More troubling is that the sites she revered have lost something. Some force field, some *duende*. They used to loom like gods. Now they seem, against logic, to have shrunk, grown dirtier, more mere. It's still and always the most beautiful city on earth, but—heresy even to suggest this—somehow the cathedrals, the great parapets, twisting passageways, sagging stone steps, mansards and domes and gargoyles don't *throb* as they once did, the way the Saint-Sulpice bells tolling the hour used to strike her, body and soul, like a gong, making her weep.

How much of all that was simply attached to memories of travel with Kirk? To the rose-colored filter of a younger gaze?

She glances at Ollie's grave face, his big ears. Before them both the long lake riffles in the wind, color of pencil lead.

Why, she thinks, do we demand that things add up?

Our peculiar burden. That's what Kirk would say. Burden and object. Dogged and dumb as a beating heart.

She thinks of her own heart, lubbing along like a deaf-mute sailor afloat in her rib cage. Quiet, faithful, rowing away. Unaware of its heart-ness, or of any limit to itself, any allotted span.

This plunges her suddenly into a terrible sadness.

She pops the last grape into her mouth, aware her lower lip is trembling. Sweet flesh bursts between her teeth; she chews slowly.

Dusts her wet hands of clinging bits of stem.

What needs to be known will pop up later. That much, at her age, you semi-trust. Bound to happen. Lifts to the surface of a sudden, like a fat orange carp. But it takes time.

Time.

There's a soundtrack for this, too. The Catalan song, guitar. "*El Noi de la Mare.*" She can play it in her head note for note. Closing of a bedtime story. Music that seems to open its hands: *And here's where it stops for now: we've come to the leaving-off place. This is the way our story goes.*

Shoves herself into a stand.

Alley-oop? she says to him, holding out her hands.

A good joke, the weather for their last day. Or so they might claim later, if they ever agree to talk about it.

Sun is blasting; sky a clear, hot blue. Almost funny, given how much cold wet gray they've endured.

Popped like pingpong balls from the Étoile métro spout they stand blinking in the heat, facing the impossibly wide street, thunderous traffic packed across countless lanes and tearing round and round the great, pocked Arc de Triomphe—towering at several blocks' distance above them. They tilt back their heads to discern T-shirted ants, moving and gesticulating along its top edges.

The two waver together on the sidewalk. Sunday afternoon. Masses of people in every direction—families *en promenade,* tourists, trinket-sellers. Young men hawking bottles of water, gypsy women shuffling up, beseeching hands held out, crosshatched palms the color of yellowed teeth. The combined noise is big, and after a few moments it becomes ambient: their heads won't ring until later.

I want to go see the monument, Fran shouts, shading her eyes. Take a few snaps. Maybe go up. Wanna come?

No thanks, Ollie hollers. You go. I'll wander around—meet you here in half an hour?

Fine, sweetie. Watch your moneybelt. And drink water. She turns and trots toward the apparition like a girl entering a fair, darting between packs of tourists—some led by guides holding pennants aloft, like parade mascots. She weaves through the gush of humankind, the red in her hair glinting.

He stands another moment, watching her.

He has no plans, no ideas: a little lightheaded to be temporarily stripped of his copilot. They've both prepacked several times for the flight home, each awake since 5:00 this morning, silently moving around each other, laying articles in piles, restacking piles. Counting down in desperate earnest, striving to act composed: the brittle, exhausted politeness that marks final hours of any trip. He'd wanted to do a last load of laundry that afternoon—he's always hated carrying dirty clothes alongside clean ones—also wanted to go through his suitcase another time, arrange things more tightly.

She refused to allow it. Are you out of your freaking *mind?* she'd boomed, facing him with popped eyes. You can do laundry at home til you turn blue. These are our last few hours in the greatest city in the world. You are coming with me.

He wouldn't have chosen this area for their last excursion. Far too crowded, too sprawling; the *magasins* frigid and posh; cinemas and kiosk posters oversized, hyper-shrill. He doesn't feel *located* anywhere along this grandest of boulevards. And though the Arc is by conventional measures magnificent, and carries a history that scarcely seems possible now, he has lost interest in pushing through mobs to commune with Greatest Hits. In fact the Arc depresses him—as do similar structures—

for its severity, its hard militarism. Murderousness seems embedded in it, entombed with it, a reminder of all the worst. Infinitely kinder are the rounded mansards, the *hôtels particulières* like layer cakes, the Henry Moore-ish statuary—anything with softer lines, anything with whimsy, like the kinetic water-sculptures near the Pompidou (the Pompidou self-important and silly, but at least it bounces light around). Though his gums have stopped bleeding and his rash gone away (as well as the needling pain in his ear, and most of the shin splints) he is badly constipated, no matter how many prunes he eats. He can feel the blockage distending his lower digestive track, bulky, uncomfortable—the apparatus stubborn and unrepentant, like some troll who's chosen this moment to stop work and leer. Ollie's skin feels clammy from trapped toxins.

The heat, though they have claimed to miss it, feels overpowering.

He retreats to the edge of the wide walk farthest from the street, backed against a pale stucco wall off of which heat bounces, cooking him from two sides.

He glances about. There are so many dark-skinned vendors of toys and trinkets he has a moment's sense he's in Morocco. At the same time, that ridiculous song named for this enormous throughway, the video Fran once sent of the skinny young slackers ambling along, singing and making who, me? faces, shrugging and mugging, plays again and again through his mind. He can't banish it, and has been half-trying, the past week, to memorize it just to amuse Fran.

Je m'baladais sur l'avenue . . . le coeur ouvert à l'inconnu . . .

He's unspeakably glad to know he'll get his life back in a day.

He'll feel then—once home again—like Dorothy after she's wakened back in Kansas. Only it won't be Kansas. It'll be a dream of comfort, of the known, a pair of slippers so well-used they've become silken casts of his feet. His own little life again. The park, the flat, the street, his Grieg. Everything in English—he's exhausted by the idioms and slang in *Paris Match* and *Le Monde*, phrases he should be able to translate for Fran but cannot without elaborate research, maddened by the slowness of that, maddened further when the words don't show up at all in his ridiculous pocket dictionary. He's sick of the acrid *froideur* of clerks, eyeing him as though he were a pestering mongrel, sick of being the petitioning fool. He'll put on *Wedding Day at Troldhaugen* first thing: it will fill his heart and lungs, and he'll commence some vigorous cleaning. Cup of tea, film at the Lumière. His own excellent coffee. His own meals. Not hemorrhaging money every minute. Going where and when he wants or not at all. No Fran in his ear every second telling him what to do, how to live.

Also, his bowels will know they've returned to the familiar. How is it bowels know these things; how is it they have their own mind this way? *Home!*, they will sing with undisguisable joy, and they will hasten to resume their tasks, eager and exuberant.

Peace. Order. *Bien-être*. He'll not take these for granted again soon.

Or so he vows. As he does, his eyes sweep the busy crowds without hope or interest, pass and then return—as if magnetized—to one of the vendors. A boy.

A very beautiful boy.

Standing in the middle of the baking sidewalk, outfitted in shapeless shirt and pants whose colors (if any there ever were) left the fabric long ago. The boy's feet—thick and wide and articulated, the feet of a population which seldom wears shoes—are dust-coated, in rubber flipflops. People stream past him on all sides. A few slow down long enough to eye the offerings set upon a piece of cloth at his feet. These are miniature Eiffel

Towers hooked to a metal loop, keychains. Tin, probably. Painted in one of three colors: gold, charcoal, silver, the paint already beginning to flake.

A propped piece of cardboard bears scrawled prices in black marker: one for two euros, three for five euros.

J'avais envie de dire bonjour à n'importe qui . . .

Ollie cannot take his eyes from the boy, a vision unlike any he can remember. Perhaps seventeen, eighteen. Hair a swath of dusty black so dense it looks carved. Skin the color of a brazil nut. Black brows shelter eyes of depthless black, nose and chin and mouth in perfect Greek proportion. The boy could be a film star—but so exotic and ungroomed he would likely be cast as a member of a marauding tribe.

Or an angel.

N'importe qui, ce fut toi . . . Je t'ai dit n'importe quoi . . .

The boy stands in full sun, squinting at nothing. Waiting. Tourists and local *promeneurs* chatter past in flocks, ignoring the small array at the boy's feet.

Ollie watches, and as if some painful dye has been injected into it his heart begins to hurt: a slow ache, radiating through his chest and arms.

Where does the boy sleep? When did he last eat, or bathe? Dozens of young men like him hustle the exact same trash not fifteen feet away, in fact all up and down the Champs-Élysées. Is there some kind of pimp controlling these kids? Doubtless they've arrived to the city like fish in a net, without money or language—the pimp must do the talking for them—perhaps the pimp has already bribed the local flics to let them sell there for the day. Likely he warns the boys what sorts of trouble to look out for, when and how to vanish. How much does the pimp collect of their pitiful daily take?

What else, dear Lord, does he ask of them?

Ollie swallows hard, holding his elbows. He stands motionless, his chest thudding and shirring.

Il suffisait de te parler . . . pour t'apprivoiser.

The boy looks out into the moving crowds without focus. He seems to have no thoughts, dull and patient as an animal, as though accustomed to standing in sun all day with little or no result.

Is it better, as Kirk used to say, than whatever he was doing where he came from?

The sight of the boy standing vacant, patient, is more than Ollie can bear. His forehead beading with moisture, he fumbles open the zipper of his money belt (soaked with sweat against his pale, distended lower belly) and extracts a damp five-euro note.

Aux Champs-Élysées . . .

In the laser heat and white light he takes a couple of steps until he faces the boy. Up close the young creature is dustier still. His eyes show more ignorance than Ollie has expected to see. Opaque, without thought or anticipation, waiting. When Ollie approaches, the boy jumps to attention, stirred that someone shows interest in the tokens. At once he kneels next to them. Without a word he gathers a set of three and carefully lifts them toward Ollie. His face concentrates on this practiced movement.

Aux Champs-Élysées . . .

Ollie's heart feels shot. The heat is so intense the sunscreen he applied earlier has melted into his eyes; they begin to sting. Rubbing them only seems to intensify the sting. Something's also begun with his stomach, a low twinge.

Cars flowing; crowds scroll past like repeating film. Horns braying in heat.

Au soleil, sous la pluie . . .

Ollie squats to examine the trinkets. He selects one; holds out the five-Euro note. The boy sees the five-note, and tries to hand Ollie the other two miniature towers. Gently, Ollie presses the extra two away; at the same time, he closes the boy's fist around the bill.

The boy's face takes a moment. Then it breaks into a smile Ollie will remember, with a knife-turn in his vitals, for the rest of his life. The smile has no complexity, no larger story. It is the sun. Ollie feels his heart crack open, and the gesture that comes next occurs without any agency at all, like leaves stirred by wind. He watches his own hand, the hand he's used to close the boy's fist around the bill, lift upward to cup itself against the boy's warm, dusty, nutbrown cheek.

À midi ou à minuit . . .

What follows happens so quickly Ollie will have difficulty—trying to think it through ten thousand times in years to come—breaking it into discrete components. The boy drops his trinkets and the freed fist shoots out like the panicked animal it is, landing against Ollie's upper cheekbone and part of his eye and nose. Ollie, who has been squatting, is pushed backward by the blow, landing on his bony ass on the cement. The surprise and pain to his right eye stuns him: his left hand automatically reaches back to stop the fall while the right flies up, in the same instant, to cover the struck quadrant of his face. With his horrified left eye he glimpses the boy, wild-eyed and lightning-quick, scoop the cloth containing his wares into a bundle, snatch up his sign and sprint off, dissolving into the crowds pushing toward the Arc as if he'd never existed.

Il y a tout ce que vous voulez aux Champs-Élysées.

Fran finds Ollie minutes later: still splayed on the sidewalk, hands over his eyes, sobbing like a preschooler in the middle of a circle of curious passers-by.

She's helped him toward the first bench they can find, its back against the avenue: a small untended park off the sidewalk, under some precious shade. The area's barren and weedy, but it must once have been a small amusement grounds: across from the bench where they sit stands a boarded-up carousel.

Ollie, please stop crying, she tells him. It's not *useful*.

He blows his nose with the wadded but clean tissue she's found, while she hurries off to find anything cold to apply to the blueblack sickle forming around his eye, colors spreading over the upper side of his nose and cheekbone. He dabs the affected nostril, stares at a pinkish discharge of blood and mucous. This interests him; also makes him queasy. He will need to find a bathroom soon: his bowels have waked up. She returns with a cold bottle of water. They take turns drinking from it. Ice, she remarks, is honest to God rarer here than diamonds.

He tells her what happened while she holds the bottle to his bruises. A slight hiccough interrupts him every couple of sentences.

She listens, holding the wet container to his eye until, annoyed, he takes it from her and holds it there himself.

I didn't mean anything by it, he whispers a second time, his eyes on the dry dirt, the creeping weeds. I only wanted to— reassure him.

Jesus, Ollie.

They're silent a minute. His heart flutters and sags, flutters and sags. He wishes he were in bed anywhere else—a million miles from here, an isolated cool bed in a dark room with no human soul around for years. Sartre was right; hell really is other people. The roar of the avenue behind them, the Sunday mobs, have blended into air.

Then Fran begins talking, legs crossed, leaning her head back against the bench; her eyes on the dry chestnut above them, the parched leaves, air still too hot for a single bird to yet show itself.

Kid was afraid, Fran is saying. That's all. Trained to be on the defensive. Probably been warned beforehand about nut-balls. I can imagine the lecture he got when he set up. Next time you'll just have to be more aware. A few friendly words might have helped, put the kid at ease. Of course he wouldn't know much French. Maybe none. Maybe you're lucky he didn't snatch off your money belt before he ran. It's always more unnerving when they're gorgeous, I know. I had a little friend like that in Africa, innocent as milk but impudent too, in his way. Tili, that was his name—wow, thought I'd forgotten that name; suddenly there it is. Underfed, of course; difficult to know his age because of that. Hard for your kid just now, too, I'm sure. Good-looking kid like that probably has to fend off dozens—

It is unbearable.

Ollie turns to look at her. Something white shoots through him.

Shut up, he says softly, trembling.

She stops, blinks at him.

What?

He draws himself to a wobbling stand and faces her, still pressing the sweating bottle to his cheek. His face has turned gray except for the storm-colored borealis around his eye, upper cheekbone and half his nose.

Do not, he says, tell me what to do. Do not tell me what this means. Do not explain my life to me or how to do it better or how you managed the same thing better somewhere else, he says.

His voice is shaking. His empty hand squeezing, squeezing.

She gapes up at him.

You, Fran, can be a selfish machine. Did you know that? Has anyone ever told you that? You mow through lives. Mow *over* them. Everything only matters when it relates to you. You don't *listen*. You answer other people's stories with stories about yourself. You dismiss everyone else as an idiot—every pore of you sends that message. You give advice because you like the idea of yourself giving advice. You enjoy watching the movie of yourself being helpful. And in the end that's all your helpfulness adds up to—you listening to yourself, admiring yourself, knowing you'll feel virtuous later. You're cruel, Fran, and reckless and condescending—don't think you can disguise that; it's obvious as a clown nose.

Oh, and I know what you think of me. Heavens yes, I've known it a long time. You think I'm neurasthenic. A neurasthenic old queen, a bowl of Jell-O. Of course I know that. But I've always kept quiet; never argued. Because I was a gentleman. Because I loved Kirk. Because I didn't want to upset you. Also because it's always exhausting for me *even to consider* arguing with you. Because that would be like shaking a wasp nest. There'd only be the next thousand arguments pouring out, to swat away. It could carry on damned well forever.

Her face and neck have turned yellowish-white, her eyes coated, glacial.

A long moment.

How dare you, she says at last.

How dare you, she says again. Can you possibly understand what it means to be with you, Ollie? Can you understand what it feels like being strapped to a grenade? I've practically run ahead of you this whole trip strewing flower petals—I've been like some fucking *groupie* for you. Draping the landscape. Pre-briefing. Running interference. Looking out, accommodating, attending, responding—holy God, the responding. Anticipating, smoothing, *soothing.* Diapering, you wanna get right down to it? Diapering. Christ help us if we don't find the acceptable *laverie,* the choicest spot in the *exactly right* café. (She pinches up her face, mocking:) *Is the paté gamy?* I hope I never see another vitamin-powder or herbal tincture or hand-sanitizer in my life. And your bathroom routines make Marcel Proust look like a linebacker.

She grips the seat of the bench with both hands. Cords stand out in her neck.

Dear God, Ollie, I've wiped your ass and patted your head. Everything, everything to *make it better.* I've been a bloody diplomat. And if by some disastrous chance you still feel miserable—and you do feel miserable most of the time, let's be very clear—well then woe unto me. My doing. My bad. I've somehow designed this cruel and fault-riddled world. I'm its shabby-ass door-to-door salesman. Expressly to torment Mr. Sensitive. Me, the *handler.* Sancho Panza to your agonized

Quixote. Do you have any conceivable idea how much work all this takes? How much psychic energy? Your face should be in the dictionary under the term *passive aggressive*.

He stands before her, quivering.

She crosses her arms as she yells. Her face and neck are covered with rash-like blotches.

And you know what else? I've only done all this, all of it, because of Kirk. Because I wanted to honor the friendship. I wanted to provide continuity. To help you get a fucking *life*. How many other real friends have you got, Ollie? Tell me. Tell me that.

He is breathing through his teeth. His heart rattles. He doesn't take his eyes from her face.

Don't hand me that, he says in low tones. You don't have any friends either, Fran. I know how you live. The people you call friends were either Kirk's friends first, or they were part of your job. Kirk's old buddies see you once a year out of guilt, some sense of civic duty. That's all. You make them feel inadequate and stupid, so they can't wait to get out of your sight. And your coworkers at the paper ditched you after you retired because they don't need you anymore. Why would they? Why, tell me, would they choose to seek you out if they didn't have to? Not many people I know—yeah, despite what a perv you think me to be—have a craving for being snubbed. Life is short. Why would they wake up in the morning and think, *wow, I really miss tucking into a big heaping plateful of disdain. Oh, and I feel the need for instruction! Someone to show me the path, the best and only way. Yessir, that's what I need. I need to call Fran!*

His shoulders seem to have crept up to his ears.

Both their chests are heaving.

Listen to me carefully, Fran. I'll say this once.

You. Can. Be. Wrong.

He clasps the now-warm bottle against his heart with both hands. A little girl and her mother, holding hands, pass at some distance: both turn their heads at the sound of Ollie's voice. The child cranes her head around after they pass to keep looking; the mother tugs her on.

Hard to imagine, yes, Ollie says. But you have been known, in your years among the living, *to be completely wrong.* Nobody calls you on it. Least of all me. I've let you browbeat me too long. All your gloating certainty! Like watching someone step off a cliff wearing a blindfold. So just keep that picture in mind, will you? Wrap your mind around that picture every time you start to open your mouth to tell everybody how to do everything.

And please bear it in mind when you do me the favor now, please, of Kindly. Shutting. Up.

He is gasping, possibly about to faint, eyes still fastened on hers as if watching a building burn down. Then he recalls something. He turns around, facing the carousel.

I have to go to the bathroom, he says, his back to her.

He stalks off to find one. If necessary, he'll use the bushes.

She sits very still, staring after him.

Good luck with that, you sick son of a bitch, she screams at his retreating form.

Then her face remembers itself, and starts to cry.

They hunch in their boarding area, facing away from each other, watching the pooling people. Light filters through the elaborate structure, a viral coagulate of glass and escalators, grayblue, like skimmed milk.

Today's *grève*, brought to them by cleaners of the plane's cabin, has delayed their flight two hours. The flight attendants have had to step in and clean. Ollie has asked a middle-aged passenger—a retired schoolteacher, about to embark on an American vacation—how they, the French, can stand the constant stoppage of crucial services this way, the slammed door of it. She shrugged. We think it's an effective action, she finally said. Also—she smiled tiredly as she said it—we are a moribund people.

Overhead announcements repeat security reminders in a breathless, lilting woman's voice. Exquisite French—like hearing jewels glitter.

Charles de Gaulle has good bathrooms, but you have to hunt for them.

Fran and Ollie stare into air, in opposite directions.

We never really ate *coq au vin,* Fran says to the air, sadly. We ate stuff sort of like it, but they never called it that. Maybe they don't call it that anymore. Maybe it's been passé for years and they call it all those other names.

I can't remember hearing anybody singing out loud, Ollie murmurs to no one. Wasn't that supposed to be the start of all this?

She makes no response. She heard a delivery man whistling once, outside the place in the Bastille where they got coffee, but she keeps silent.

They watch the parading passengers-to-be. Some talk idly, having run out of subjects. Others sit listless, siphoned out. Skin with no contents. *Crevé,* thinks Ollie. Excellent word. Three quarters of the people here—like themselves—resemble flat tires.

For what is the body, Ollie thinks, but another kind of bag, toting guts from place to place?

And why (he follows this thought dreamily) do we want to tote ourselves around?

To see what we can see.

At once, the chorus from the kids' campfire song echoes like a taunt. *To see what we can see. To see what we can see.* And what was it, in the original tune—after all that going-over-the-mountain—that the curious bear had finally seen?

Why, *the other side of the mountain.*

That had been the song's payload. A comedy tagline, spritz-in-the-face. And that payload had indeed struck him, when he was a kid, as splendidly funny. *Good one, huh? Because come on now—what did you honestly think the bear would find?*

They haven't spoken much since the blowup.

Separately, they'd made their ways back to the hotel room.

There, after an hour of silence, moving past each other like zombies, making motions of last-minute packing (though they'd already repacked many times) Fran had abruptly apologized, and with piteous eyes told him he was right about every single thing he'd said. This would have seemed facile to Ollie, a cop-out, even another form of condescension—except for her eyes, which held a crushed quality he could barely bring himself to look at. He had forced his mouth to hold shut so as not to blurt the automatic fix—the apology, the admission of sins. He'd said nothing at all. It took every ounce of will he owned to manage that.

Then there'd been nothing to say.

They'd watched television, commercials of beautiful young Frenchwomen emerging from crystal pond water half nude to take a bite of candy or yogurt, or drink from a tiny bottle of Orangina. They went back to the Café de Lyon for supper, ate in silence—*steak frites* and *poulet frites* now generic standbys—from all appearances two prisoners of a dead-end marriage. They filed back in silence to their room, set the alarm for a horribly early hour to be ready for the horribly early cab, and crept into their beds. Neither slept. Today their eyes wear blue crescents under them, except for Ollie's right eye, whose concentric rings range in shades from charcoal to jade green.

For no reason except maybe to pass time, they've begun to list disappointments aloud.

No one will care what happened to us here when we get back, she says after a minute. Nobody gives a fuck what we saw or what we ate. They'd rather tough out an attack of hives than see our photos. I know that's the way I feel when people come back *cockadoodle-doo*ing about their amazing time in Samarkand or Kyle of Lochalsh or Namibia. I only want them to go away and shut up—

She stops, appalled she's just fulfilled one of Ollie's observations about her. But he's too glum to notice.

There seems no point to describing any of it after the fact, he agrees.

The two watch families, business people, students. Buzz, buzz. Everyone wears lots of rumpled hair, Kennedylike. Parents look dazed and heroic.

It won't matter to anyone except us, she continues. It will disappear from the screen in minutes, seconds. Like Facebook. Probably we'll want to forget the whole thing ourselves, fast as we can.

He has no reply.

A minute passes. She sinks her chin into her hands.

I miss Mexican food, she says.

3

And now at last, he's got them back again.

The days he missed. The life he missed. Or maybe, misplaced.

The *bien-être.*

Why not indulge his vision? No one else needs to know. He is a modern Rilke, making his way modestly under the radar. The consolation? Simple daily rounds. Excellent mind, rearer of small children, lover of art. It will take many years, long after he's gone, for the unapprised public to realize—full of wonder—he was amongst them. Hah. Meantime his obscurity is his serenity, his protection. *Imagine: Ollie Gaffney used to walk this path to the park every day.*

He clambers up the weed-lined path in wide, practiced strides, past the redwoods and cypresses, through the brush and dead pine needles. All he needs is a walking stick. Didn't Rilke use one? And a *pince-nez.*

The book's clamped in his armpit, a copy of *Malte Laurids Brigge,* found for a mere six dollars in the delightful used section of Green Apple. (Oh, the heavenly smell inside that splintering store. Must, mildew, dust, millions of yellowed, crackling old pages.) Stephen Mitchell translation—fondness for Mitchell, local fellow, Berkeley, did the *Tao Te Ching*. Ollie's pasted a sticky-note beside the quote he loves:

> ... *What a happy fate, to sit in the quiet room of an ancestral house, among calm, sedentary Things, and to hear the wrens trying out their first notes in the airy, bright-green garden, and far away the chimes of the village clock. To sit and look at a warm streak of afternoon sun ... if I could have lived some-where, anywhere in the world, in one of the many closed-up country houses that no one cares about. I would have used just one room (the bright room in the attic), and I would have lived there with my old Things, the family portrait, the books. I would have had an armchair and flowers and dogs and a strong walking stick for the stony paths. And nothing else. ...*

Ollie prefers to skip the short paragraph to follow. It's depressing, and really doesn't apply.

> *But life has turned out differently. God knows why. My old furniture is rotting in the barn where I left it, and I myself, yes, my God, I have no roof over me, and it is raining into my eyes.*

Ah but no no no, none of that: *pas du tout.*

He lives—for all purposes—in the bright room in the attic. That's right. Among calm, sedentary Things. The family portrait exists in his head, in detail. The books were always there. And today the warm streak of afternoon sun's already burning away the mist, eucalyptus acorns squashed fragrantly over the earth.

Since the day of re-entering his flat he's been beside himself, all but waltzing. Everything he gazes upon welcomes him, begs to be petted, celebrated. Exactly like Ebenezer after the four ghosts shook him up. The streets, the grubby walks, the Russian fog, grimed storefronts, the grinning Asian gentleman who shouts his name when he stops in with his drycleaning—even the screaming garbage trucks on Thursday mornings, sounding like dinosaurs in combat.

The smell of coffee from the dozen cafés along Irving, along Ninth. The smell of seafood from the oyster place, garlic from the decrepit Italian eatery with the flip-page jukebox gizmos still at each table. The familiar crazy man, bald, ruddy, potbellied in his oversized clothes, talking and laughing to himself along Judah.

All inexpressibly dear.

He forgets to read the obituaries in the morning. He goes straight to the arts pages, or to the Magazine. He likes the weekly Lives column. It makes him feel there is constant, arbitrary, inexplicable strangeness in the world. With that as a given, how can he can be doing badly?

Even the slippery little fish of panic has quieted at night. Not entirely gone, but swimming slower, like it's doped. He waits, marking its passage. After it settles he switches off the light. It's conceivable he could actually grow fond of it after this much time together. A personal pet. Minimal maintenance. (He chuckles, making his way up the rise.)

And the peace! Ho!

Fran has not contacted him except for the single e-mail she sent right after they landed, noting she'd reached home safely. No embellishment. Nothing since. No reviews, articles, jokes; no upbraiding, no bulletins.

Yes, velvet peace. Exempting of course the garbage trucks and sirens (so familiar he's almost stopped hearing them). Today, the nasal, annoyed yammer of squirrels. Also of course the red-winged blackbirds, whose quarrelsome song and flash of fiery wingsplotch—he's elated to notice—have not changed a bit. His own *wrens trying out their first notes in the airy, bright-green garden.* Neither, thankfully, has the scent of eucalyptus changed, the huff-huffing runners, the laughing, shining dogs on morning maneuvers—setters, lab retrievers, spaniels, Scotties, their fur bouncing—nor the occasional tantalizing whiff of someone's cigarette or pipe tobacco—

But what is this?

He's been covering ground fast, scanning the pine needles, not looking up. And when at last he does, a man is sitting upon his—Ollie's—bench.

Smack in its center, as if he owns it. The man is reading, an ankle propped on a knee.

Of course it's happened on occasion in the past that someone's occupied his bench, but not usually this early. It's eight-thirty in the morning.

Ollie stops perhaps ten feet from the man, and his jaw must be hanging because the man looks up, shuts his book over one hand, and smiles.

Hello, says the man. Would you like to sit here, too?

The man's voice modulates the phrase like notes of a guitar.

Ollie opens his mouth, but his voice won't come.

By all means, the man urges. Please, he says, scooting leftward, patting the space beside him on the bench.

Well—ah—thank you, croaks Ollie at last in a tone that very much doubts this to be a good idea. He approaches the bench with care, turning his back to it at the last moment and placing his bottom on the designated spot as if it is strapped with explosives. The man watches, smiling more broadly. Ollie must be supplying him great entertainment. Of course Ollie longs to race away; better yet just disappear this second into air. But in the bright spotlight of the man's graciousness—almost blinding—he can't think up an inoffensive way to decline.

The man has crew-cut silver hair, a close-trimmed silver goatee, and spectacles. His brows and lashes are dark, eyes also dark as espresso; pupil and iris indistinguishable. His eyes and manner are kind and (Ollie can't stop noticing) hugely amused. He wears chocolate-colored safari shorts and a gray cotton T-shirt bearing a Buffalo Springfield logo. His feet, without socks, are encased in red high-top sneakers.

Ollie can't pull his eyes from the high-tops. High-tops gave him supreme happiness as a kid. Something about the ankle support. He'd felt so buttressed, so *capable* in them.

He also cannot help noticing the man is tall and well-made. The man's arms are shapely in their T-shirt sleeves. His stomach is flat, legs long, fine goldish down over his calves and forearms. He is brown in a sunned way. He appears relaxed inside his skin.

Hugo Summerfield, says the man, extending his hand.

Ollie grasps the hand. It is warm, dry, strong.

Oliver—Ollie—Gaffney, he finishes weakly.

The cotton sky, the shredding mist, gentle eucalyptus—crowding, crowding close like a photographer's shroud. Ollie's vision seems to have shrunk to the field of a child's telescope, a silver-dollar-sized lens brimming with the long form and delighted face of Hugo Summerfield.

A pleasure, Ollie. What's the book? Hugo points at the volume still mashed under Ollie's left arm.

Ollie's forgotten it's there.

Oh.

He unclamps the book from his armpit, horrified it may be damp where it was pressed in.

He tries surreptitiously to fan at it once or twice before showing the cover to Hugo.

Brigge! Hugo tilts his face to shout at the sky, and when the face returns it is grinning as if it had run into a dear old friend from high school—which, Ollie will later reflect, the book must almost certainly be.

Love him, Hugo says. He's really the crown prince, isn't he? Glorious work, this one. Under-acknowledged now. Can't own too many editions of it, he adds, leaning conspiratorially toward Ollie, tapping the book as he says this. As if he not only assumes a world of erudition inside Ollie, but also *confers* that world with an intimate twinkle. As if the two of them are seasoned cognoscenti, relishing a cognoscenti secret.

Ollie gapes. Somewhere in his mind the term *crown prince* strums like a chord. It is just right, he thinks.

A seagull soars above them, *scree-scree*ing. The cool salt of ocean smells near.

After a moment Hugo says: And here is mine. Removing the place-saving hand—unfazed, presumably, by the task of relocating his page—he holds forth the book he was absorbed in when Ollie stumbled up. Like *Brigge* it is an old hardback, a color that might have once been tomato, binding worn through, criss-crossed with bare white threads. The title's embossed in the middle, in dull gold.

Twenty-Thousand Leagues Under the Sea.

Ollie looks from the cover to Hugo, twice.

That is the first movie I ever saw, he whispers.

The fig tree Kirk planted has thickened while she was away. Amazing how fast. So full she can scarcely see into the kitchen window of the frat house next door.

In little over a month, the tree's become a jungle of fat green leaves—lurid, shiny. Dense as plates. You have to bend and twist to find any triangle of viewable space between them.

Makes matters difficult for a voyeur. Or is it voyeuse? She stands at the bedroom window, drying her eyeglasses with tissue.

She'd never considered, when Kirk put in the stripling, that it might take over the narrow band of turf between the houses. Neither had he. Weirdly, the thing never fruits right. Green, vessel-shaped fruit pops forth, bright and promising—then stops growing midway, never ripening. Still, the tree booms from the ground like Jack's beanstalk, branching, densifying. Maybe its root system will start crowding the foundation of the house. But how to stop what's so powerfully under way?

Trees have their own minds. Maybe this will be the fruiting year.

She peers at the white-ish sky. Big heat coming today. Morning warns you. A series of tasks. Throw open all the doors and windows early. Seal them shut by noon; turn on every ceiling fan. Sit still or sleep, or flee the house for somewhere air conditioned until six or so, then throw everything open again. The old house acts like a mud oven, holding the cool til afternoon, then pregnant til late evening with crazy heat. Cold showers still help, just as always. She used to beg Kirk to install cooling, but he insisted a few weeks of heat every year wasn't the worst. She felt he was being cheap then. Now she can't be bothered.

She leans a moment against the window frame. Misses scratching her forehead and cheek against the wiry file of his beard, his caramel smell, stretched out beside her. His vast patience. She felt like a horse rubbing its cheek along a rough fence. His gaze would lapse into space while she did this; she could never help asking what he was thinking—imagining, of course, he'd made some profound philosophical breakthrough. His answer would be something so homely and prosaic they'd both fall down laughing. Like, Did you ever realize that we can see the refrigerator from where we are here on the bed? Or: Should we have small red potatoes with rosemary and garlic, or polenta with asiago? He would knead her right shoulder—the computering shoulder that was always sore, and she'd groan with relief.

She misses his own mysterious little groan into his towel, when he dried his face after his shower. She thought it had something to do with the relieving pressure on his eyes, also the longing not to have to wake up. In all their years, she never asked him what that little groan meant. It seemed too private.

When they were just starting out, he'd written her a poem. She's still got it somewhere—probably the bottom of a box. The poem mentioned some of the strange, un-alike adventures of both their early lives, and ended with the lines: *Ah love, who knows just why it is / we do the things we do? / Perhaps so we can have someone / to tell it to.*

Anticipating the heat, she's already watered front and back, hydrangeas, camellias, rabbit ears, mint (*See, honey? I've kept them alive*), gazing awhile at the starburst agapanthas, whose lavender precisely matches that of the potato vine blossoms covering the trellis around the porch. Kirk hadn't planned that either, but he'd have liked it a lot.

The house, as always, is silent.

She used to beg Kirk for silence. For no plans, no visitors. Implored him. *Warm oil in the ear.*

Nothing at all—she'd known it would be the case—has happened in the wake of her trip with Ollie. Mail collected, most of it trash. Late notices on library books. She's seen a few people in the supermarket, the drugstore, the gym. They make convivial noises, eyes cautious. Fran nods pleasantly, sends them on. She says nothing about her travels. The world is one of those moving walkways at the airport—rolling, steady, flat, without mind.

The silent house.

Music is wanted. She walks to the kitchen and clicks on the boombox. At once the classics station peals from the speakers—a default position; she likes to check what the station is doing before selecting her own. This morning it's the famous Bach movement—in truth it only became famous after appearing (like a character, she thinks) in the William Hurt film, *Children of a Lesser God.* (Christ he looks young in those video excerpts. Nearly a child.) Concerto in D Minor for Two Violins, second movement. She can never hear the piece without stopping what she is doing and dropping into a chair. If she's driving, she pulls over. But it's not only the Bach anymore that does this. It's "Foggy Mountain Breakdown" and "Embraceable You" and "Guantanamera." It's *Finlandia. Scheherezade.* Caetano Veloso. Torroba. *Black Orpheus.* It's Motown, Buddy Holly, Sam Cooke. "Some Enchanted Evening," "*Nessun Dorma*"—it's fucking "America the Beautiful." And the Brazilians, never forget the Brazilians. If someone's made a time capsule of recordings to speak on behalf of Earth, please let Debussy be in there. Of course it's all of Mozart: what being, even made of nails, could stand unmoved by the Requiem, or the Cavatina from *Marriage of Figaro.* Whatever is playing will uncannily describe the world to hand—whether it's rain or roadkill or Girl Scouts selling cookies or miles upon miles of gridlocked traffic.

Only lately, she begins to wonder what the music is trying to tell her.

This is it, the music begs. *Take me in. There's no time. Take me in.*

Her eyes roam to the old Christmas ornament hanging by the window. A red velvet hexagonal star stitched with gold piping and sequins, gold tassel for a tail. Fine dust covers it. She'd thought it pretty and tacked it there one Christmas, and later Kirk said *but the holiday's over, don't you want to take it down,* and she'd said no, she liked it there, and there it has hung, motionless, Christ knows how many years. Nothing changes or moves in this house now, unless she moves it.

I'm all we've got, the music repeats, like some desperate SOS hammered out over and over from an unknown planet.

Take me in. She drops her head, letting the music soak through.

What does it want of her? What does it want her to do?

n late October, as the air begins to hint of cooler currents, of pepper and vanilla and other plans, Ollie receives his first call from Fran since they resumed their American lives.

It's a blissful time in the city, sunny and clear, afternoons buttery.

Butter-light falls across the side table in the bedroom where the phone sits, singing. He's already wearing his specs from the reading he was doing, so he can see her name on the receiver as the machine, robotic, tinka-tinks its little song. He's changed the ringtone, at Hugo's urging, to the opening theme of Beethoven's *Pastorale,* the *Allegro ma non troppo.*

He stares at Fran's name.

The air is scented with caramel tea, freshly made. Hugo found the little package of leaves from Mariage Frères (one of Ollie's forgotten Paris souvenirs) while organizing the kitchen— shouted *Yes!* and at once brewed a pot, exultant.

So much seems to thrill Hugo. Tea. Weather. Food. Ollie.

What makes you sad? Ollie has already asked him more than once. What makes you angry?

Hugo looks at him evenly each time. The usuals, he says. The worst we can be. The worst we can do. But that's a rabbit hole, isn't it. So I try (taking Ollie's chin, smiling as though Ollie were a case in point) to focus on the best. Or the better. Plenty of that too, no?

Hugo is not a reformer.

Thank every star. Ollie couldn't have borne it. He's more a calming agent, laying a hand on Ollie's arm, speaking in patient tones.

He is also, as it turns out, something of an epicure, and he's wasted no time taking over the kitchen. Cleaning, dumping, restocking. Cursing and laughing when he finds a twelve-year-old jar of mint jelly or ancient taco sauce, both petrified to black crust. Hugo reads recipes in bed at night aloud to Ollie—shows him the photos; Ollie begging him to stop because it makes him ravenous—then sets out next day to recreate them. He arrives back with grocery bags crackling, and the two set to work. Ollie's kitchen has never seen such commotion. Ollie doesn't know what else to do, so he selects background jazz. He favors mainstreamers, the MJQ, Paul Desmond, Cal Tjader, but Hugo's been infiltrating with exotica. A young Senegalese woman, Sam Cooke, Alison Krauss. A guitarist who plays only Beatles covers.

Is it possible to say it, even silently in his head, without hexing his luck?

Hugo is a keen, artful lover.

Not rough, but certainly big. And strong. He has a way of slipping up from behind unannounced, wrapping his warm, clean arms (their fine gold down) around Ollie's shoulders, planting his mouth against Ollie's neck or cheek or ear.

It had been so long, Ollie wept the first few times. Hugo held him each time, until he could weep no more. Then they'd get up to make dinner.

To borrow Fran's vulgar parlance, the whole *événement* is a fucking miracle. Anything—*any least thing*, Ollie has told himself over and over—could have checked it, prevented it. He could have chosen not to visit the park that morning. He could have tramped over an hour later. He could have chosen to turn on his heels the moment Hugo patted the bench seat, smiling like Alice's cat—and run off as fast as he knew how.

Who pulls such strings? *Personne.* No one. It's cosmic roulette.

In this case, benign. Better than benign.

And of course, Hugo is not perfect. He reads science fiction, for one thing.

He reads everything. *Un vrai type.* He reads sports, history, poetry, strange old botany manuals ferreted from the bargain bins. (He says he loves the illustrations.) But he reads science fiction and fantasy, too. Ollie, in keeping with the spirit of non-reform, refrains from comment when he glimpses the titles open in Hugo's lap, titles involving magic, time travel, and obscure, intricate kingdoms. Does Ollie imagine, during those glimpses, a tiny twiggle of mirth dancing at the corners of Hugo's mouth, though his lover's eyes are still glued to the page?

Also, Hugo badgers Ollie to go salsa dancing.

They do not yet wish to live together. They've talked about it. There's no hurry, and this feels to Ollie like a great spaciousness. Hugo taught at City College before he switched to programming in San Jose—had the luck and wits to clear out just before the famous bubble burst, taking with him a superb nest egg: he lives on its interest. Dwelt ever since in a flat in Noe Valley, just over the hill from the Sunset. (His friends up and down 24th Street are meeting Ollie one by one: the kids behind the counter in the ice cream place, in Bernie's for coffee, the bartenders at Valley Tavern, the pizza staff at Patxi's.) Both men enjoy the conscious stagings of the back and forths, the outings, the little satchels. They also—both admit—like the spells of reflection in between. Hugo, his eyes fond, calls it the Para-Migration. Their time together already forms a corpus in Ollie's mind, a growing body of work—but also warm-blooded proof of something Ollie has never known, understood, or even dreamed possible the whole of his long, dutiful life:

Fun.

They were pedaling furiously one late morning through the Presidio, single file along the cliff road toward the Palace of Fine Arts through patches of cold fog—just beginning to recede at that hour, disclosing a wrinkled lapis ocean and green-frosted Marin hills across the bay—and the great russet-colored bridge, towertops piercing fog like a couple of ladders into heaven, shimmering alongside—when the awareness made a *ping* that jolted Ollie's helmeted skull.

He stopped the bike, unstrapped the helmet, caught his breath on trembling legs.

Hugo, pedaling about thirty feet ahead, glanced back, saw his sweetheart halted by the road, long legs planted like poles on either side of his bike, staring into his helmet. Hugo stopped.

What is it? What's the matter? Hugo hollered back.

Ollie looked up at him, bewildered.

I'm having *fun,* he yelled.

Some days, like today, they just read together.

The Pastorale tinkles on, antic and unyielding, like an ice

cream truck. In the living room, Hugo, from his station on the couch, calls out: Do you plan to answer that?

Ollie doesn't respond, gazing at Fran's name. After another moment he leans to grasp the receiver.

It's me, she says softly.

Yes, he says.

A beat.

How are you, Fran?

Not bad. Not bad. Best time of year up here these days, remember. Leaves going berserk now. Well, best and worst time, really. Like Dickens, she adds with a sad little laugh.

And you, Ollie? How're you managing?

He pauses. Really well right now, Fran. Wonderfully well.

A small silence.

Ollie, I'm—so glad to hear that. Truly, I am.

The confusion in her voice, its pang of redoubled loneliness, slips a needle into his heart. He longs to pour reassurance over her; he feels his mouth open and his chest inhale to do it. But he catches himself, and keeps silent.

Another pause.

I called to invite you to something, Ollie.

The punctured heart tightens. He tries to steady his voice: attentive, reasonable.

Yes?

I'm part of something new these days, something I like. I want you to come see—come listen, she corrects herself.

She tells him the coordinates. A campus auditorium, the college where Kirk used to teach.

I won't say more, she says. Wanna surprise you.

That sounds fine, Fran. Thanks. I'll check my calendar and get back to you. And Frannie, another thing?

Yes, Ollie?

If I come, I'd—I'd like to bring someone. Would that be acceptable?

An intake of breath at the other end. He's thrown her, utterly.

Oh, Ollie. That would be just—smashing. That would be—yes. Fantastic.

He finds himself more undone than he imagined he'd be. Even after the hottest shower he can stand, his hands feel cold.

Hugo has offered to drive. A mercy: Hugo owns the better car. The night is black, moon yet to appear, stars in hiding. November, days of gray austerity before Thanksgiving. The men wear mufflers.

Hugo drives an electric-blue Honda Fit. As a special indulgence, he had leather seatcovers installed when he bought it. It's an *adult car*, Hugo has gently reminded him—unlike Ollie's dessicated Morris. Ollie scarcely uses the Morris anymore, except to move it on streetcleaning days. Though Hugo has been kind to him about it, Ollie knows the hour is nearing when they'll have to come to terms: Ollie will need to trade up, find a sturdier, more practical vehicle.

Unless they decide to consolidate.

Meantime, he loves being driven: freedom to dream, sight-see, track thoughts aloud with Hugo or not, as he pleases. In the backseat they've placed an enormous autumn bouquet (Peruvian lilies, protea, yellow mums, red and gold sunflowers) wrapped in clear cellophane, and a six pack of Maximus, Fran's favorite ale, packed into a styrofoam cooler, with ice.

Hugo had expressed concern about the six-pack. Wouldn't champagne or wine be more appropriate?

Trust me, Ollie had answered.

Since her call, he's parceled out the stories to Hugo: himself and Ennis. Hugo had listened sadly and said at the last: Everyone, sooner or later, has an Ennis. Then Ollie had told Hugo about himself and Kirk. Then about himself and Fran and Kirk—finishing tonight, in the car, with the *coup de grâce*: himself and Fran, the past year, the silence that followed. He has tried to be fair—tried to tell it in a way that makes him not sound like a jackass, describing their strange *denouement* in Paris.

Maybe not *denouement,* exactly.

More like a showdown, you ask me, Hugo says, chuckling. Gunslingers, high noon.

Then, glancing at Ollie's face: Oh, honey, I'm sorry. I know it's not funny to you. Still, she sounds alive to me, Ollie. And to me it sounds—underneath all the rest of it?—like she only wanted to help you.

Ollie stares out the window. Fields, hills, swallowed by night. There's a dairy somewhere out there to the left, but in the darkness nothing can be seen. The air's reporting it heavily, though: pungent cow manure and hay.

I suppose, Ollie murmurs.

Ollie feels Hugo's gaze—can see, even turned away from

him, the faint aura of white dashboard light tracing Hugo's half-turned profile, bouncing off his driving glasses; behind them the soft, deep, long-lashed eyes, the silvered cheeks.

You're still furious, Hugo says quietly.

The car hums through the starless black.

They follow their Google Map instructions, straining forward and sideways, heads out the window in the briny chill, to identify landmarks in the dark.

Hugo idles the car at the entrance gate to feed a five-dollar bill into a machine; the long striped arm lifts, and he pops back in to zip them through. They pull into a slot near the auditorium, where they're pleased to find a tribe of parked vehicles—more pulling up, passengers slamming out of their cars—as the two gather the wrapped flowers from the backseat.

They decide to leave the beer in the car for now. Hugo hoists the flowers.

They pace the campus: grass black in the darkness, moist and fragrant underfoot. They pass old Greekish buildings covered with vines; others newer, reflecting streetlights in long glass panes. All but the theater they move toward are shadowed, sleeping. Around and near them, people walk. Talk and laughter floats up, muted, into the sky. A pilgrimage, a genial flow. The men fall in with it.

Ollie inhales deeply; his chest tight. On the exhale he sighs:

It always smells so clean and sweet up here. Especially at night. I'd sort of forgotten.

Maybe we should think about spending a little more time up here, Hugo says.

In Ollie's belly, blorpy shapes congeal and somersault.

Maybe, he answers.

•

And now they're seated in the warm, noisy theater, halogen lights like milk over faces and bodies buzzing up and down the shallow steps, row upon row. Ollie and Hugo stash the bouquet lengthwise under their two seats; they settle in to study the crowd—a stew of ages and ethnicities, though whites predominate. Families have brought children; some look as though they skateboarded here, parents included. College kids move past in twos and threes; teachers must have promised extra credit for attending. The men smell a whiff of pot on the evening air. Several bikers carry their helmets. Elders with canes plant careful feet.

The buzzing is the hearty, expectant kind.

Hugo elbows him: Look at those two. Ollie follows his eyes several rows forward: a couple of older men sit together, perhaps in their seventies, even eighties. They're slim, composed. White hair cut close; good sweaters in salmon, absinthe. One turns to say words into the other's ear; draws a brief nod—movements so subtly entrenched it's clear at once they've been together many years.

That'll be us someday, Hugo whispers. *Disastrous* sweater colors, though.

Ollie looks at Hugo, feeling his throat close. It's not a good time for this, not a good time at all; his heart already wrought, loosed and banging against its cage bars.

Could you please be less of a saint for awhile, he wants to bawl. Instead he only pats the top of Hugo's long knee.

The lights fade, audience murmurs dissolve to silence, and in pure dark from the direction of the empty stage comes the sound of mass movement, shuffling.

Several spotlights open onto the stage, now revealing a shell-shaped gathering of perhaps forty men and women standing abreast on graduated tiers—Ollie'd paid no attention to the tiers earlier, when the house was lit. The assembled group—teenaged to snow-haired—face a lone woman whose back is to the audience, her silhouette just visible in the rim of the light.

They're smiling at her, and she, apparently, at them. All wear white shirts, and over that some sort of shiny silk smock, royal blue.

The conductor turns to face the audience, and the spotlight finds her. She's a youngish, plumpish woman with an animated face—the sort with three kids in elementary school, Ollie thinks; the sort who never forgets to bring the donuts or the oranges, who volunteers to sign for the hearing impaired. She bows, grinning, and the audience, given permission, bursts into fevered applause; whoops of recognition, shouts of encouragement bursting from different sections of the hall. *Go Rebecca! Yah, Charlie!* The individuals named grin blindly into the light, and wave.

There's Fran! Ollie whispers, his heart thunking violently as if he himself were onstage. There she is! he says, pointing for Hugo.

Fran smiles with the others at their conductor, copper curls bright against blue silk.

The whole tableau could be some high school graduation.

She looks nice, Hugo says. Pretty hair.

Ollie pins his clutched hands between his knees.

The conductor raises her arms, hums a key, bobs her arms higher, then down in an arc.

They open with the "Evening Prayer" from Humperdinck's *Hansel and Gretel*.

The chorale's voices—they sing in German, and though Ollie doesn't know German he knows the translation—hold the pure melody of the first bar, then quickly range apart into rich harmony, like melting colors. At the first notes, which Ollie has known since he was very small—listening, in awe, to his father's Metropolitan Opera broadcasts on Saturday mornings—all the follicles on his neck and scalp raise up to form pinprick points, and his eyes fill without a second's preamble. Perhaps it is shameful, but the images embodied in the ascending notes—the brave faith of two frightened children—always held the ability to stab him, and the sob that rises to consume him catches just behind his larynx.

> *Zweie, die mich decken,*
> *Zweie, die mich wecken,*
> *Zweie, die mich weisen,*
> *Zu Himmels-Paradeisen*

He drops his head low; lets the tears stream.

At once a familiar hand is upon his two—still knotted between his knees in anguish. The hand squeezes, and after a moment withdraws and returns with a clean handkerchief.

Ollie buries his face in it.

The chorale skims the musical map, changing up radically each time you think you have them categorized. They do "Java Jive." They do "Bess, You Is My Woman Now." "Don't Stand So Close to Me." *Salve Regina.* "Hurry Sundown." They do Laura Nyro—Hugo grips his knee and he grips back: *I'll never hear the bells.* They do Carole King's "Song of Long Ago," and Ollie feels something in him give way.

> *As it began, so I will end it*
> *Singing a song of long ago*
> *Loving the people I've befriended*
> *And singing a song of long, long, long ago*

They do Rogers and Hart: "It Never Entered My Mind." They sing "Steal Away," and Ollie feels gooseflesh down his legs.

Then, with no warning, the lights cut. Intermission.

The house, stunned a moment, explodes into yelling and

applauding; after a minute the milk-lights snap back on. Yelling abates to buzz. People stand to stretch and find the restrooms.

He and Hugo turn to blink at each other.

Well, Jesus Christ, Hugo says. Who knew? Did you?

Not me, Ollie says through the hanky still held to his nose, his eyes large and wet.

Not a clue, he says. She always loved music—quite madly really. But she never really sang a note during any of the time I was with her, and otherwise—

Ollie stops talking.

The handkerchief drops. His eyes go inside themselves.

Tell me something, Ollie. When was the last time you heard anyone going around whistling or singing, for no obvious reason?

Wow, Ollie murmurs, staring at the empty stage. She did it. She followed it through.

Hugo looks at him sharply. Followed what through? Hugo asks. What are you talking about?

Long story, Ollie mutters, grabbling again for Hugo's hanky, rising to a stand. Tell you later. He blows his nose with a goose-honk.

Hugo regards him intensely as he stands, starts to speak, thinks better of it.

They enter the streaming crowd, letting it carry them down the steps and out of the building through the double doors, dispersing like a fanning river into the spicy air. Both look up to see a colossal moon, low, gauzed, the same moon that shines upon Europe and Asia and Africa, the wide seas and both Poles—but here it seems to belong to the wine country over which it floats, a gentle veiled custard, silver clouds parted on either side of it like gates made of lace.

They walk silently, fists in pockets. Hugo goes off in search of the toilet.

Ollie paces fiercely, hugging himself in the cold. He cannot let this, this—sappy delirium—take over. It will disappear in an hour, like New Year's Eve confetti. Guaranteed. But before it does, it will make him agree to something he'll regret. Maybe several somethings.

He will behave foolishly.

And afterward she'll still be Fran. She'll drive him mad. She'll drink his blood.

But what else? his brain retorts.

He doesn't have to live with her. He lives with—well, not technically. Not yet. But close. Almost.

She is Kirk's wife. It's been enough time that he should be able to carry himself with some *élan*.

And if he doesn't take hold of this—if he won't let this take hold of him, while it's here before him—what's the point?

What's the point of anything?

He makes a small sound. *Ahh, gaaahd.* Flings his head back to beg the tender moon.

At which moment—like a tall genie—Hugo manifests, features cloaked in moonshadow, touching his arm.

Ready, monsieur?

That's just it, Ollie answers sadly. I'm never ready. I'll never be ready.

Shaking his head, Hugo takes his elbow.

Inside, warm and moist, smells of soap and beer and supper-breath. When the singers re-enter the stage one by one to file into the tiers, a great uproar of shouting and stamping at once fills the hall. Despite himself and with no premonition of it, Ollie leaps up as the group appears, cupping his hands around his mouth: *Fran! Fran!* She hears her name and her face darts up toward the sound. When she catches sight of him she shades her eyes from the spotlights and smiles: she waves, a bit shyly.

Her squint flicks to either side of him, and Ollie knows she is trying to identify Hugo.

She's trying to see who you are, Ollie tells Hugo.

Excellent! Hugo grins his starry grin and jumps from his chair, waving crazily with both arms. Squinting, she waves and grins back.

Clearly a woman of taste. An exceptional woman, Hugo remarks, seating himself.

Silence as the lights dim. The chorale launches into Stephen Stills's "It Doesn't Matter," from the far-back days of Manassas. Hugo goes rigid, grasping Ollie's upper arm with both hands. This is Hugo's era, Ollie knows—his secret shrine. Though Ollie's never asked, it is possible Hugo once had a crush on Stills.

(Even if this proves true, Ollie can't feel badly. In the first place, of course who wouldn't have a crush on the enchanting young Stills. In the second, the height difference would have presented serious problems.)

> *Moment by moment*
> *One day at a time*
> *It doesn't matter*
> *It's nothin' but dreamin' anyhow*

I cannot believe this, Hugo hisses into Ollie's ear. When the song ends Hugo stands, shouting while he claps.

They do Zydeco. They do South American. They do Broadway. They do American folk. They do Paul Simon, "The Only Living Boy in New York." As its finale the group commences "For All We Know": clean, unembroidered, chords and melody straight up and down as if the old jazz standard were a hymn. Then Fran slips from between her fellow choristers and steps forward to solo in a clear, uninflected alto.

So love me . . . tonight
Tomorrow was made for some;
Tomorrow may never come
For all we know—
For—all—we—know

An encore is demanded. Someone produces a Jew's harp, and someone else one of those nested spoons you whack against your thigh that makes a tickety-tick, and the group belts the traditional bluegrass ditty:

Got me the left hind leg of a rabbit
Things are comin' my way
All I have to do is just reach out and grab it
Things are comin' my way

Oh Lord, how good I feel
I come possession of a automobile
I can eat chicken and I don't have to steal,
Things are comin' my way!

The hall is on its feet. Everyone's yelling. Conductor and chorale bow and grin. In the bedlam the singers turn to one another, high-five and embrace—Fran is hugged again and again, Ollie notes. He watches her hug back hard, long, eyes shut tight.

I should ask her if she wants help—haul the bougainvillea back up onto the porch again—before the first serious frost. Could happen any minute.

Then: *Must remember to get the bouquet out from under our seats.*

And not forget the beer out of the backseat.

Then, like a set of keys given up for lost, materializing whole from nowhere, polished and shiny in the dark:

You kids get off my lawn!

—and he feels his face open. Performers and conductor turn toward the audience and start applauding them, holding their arms out to the cheering mob: you, you. The din is overwhelming, people shrieking, clapping. Someone's throwing daisies and what appear to be miniature candy bars, leftovers from Halloween, onto the stage. And now Hugo does something Ollie has never known him capable of, nor seen him do. He puts two forefingers to his mouth, and produces a hall-splitting whistle.

JUNIPER
JUNIPER PRIZE FOR FICTION

This volume is the thirteenth recipient
of the Juniper Prize for Fiction,
established in 2004 by the
University of Massachusetts Press
in collaboration with the
UMass Amherst MFA Program
for Poets and Writers, to be
presented annually for an outstanding
work of literary fiction. Like its sister award,
the Juniper Prize for Poetry established
in 1976, the prize is named in honor
of Robert Francis (1901–1987),
who lived for many years at
Fort Juniper, Amherst, Massachusetts.